"THE STORY TAKES OFF LIKE A ROCKET.
GOOD FUN AND JOLLY HAIR-RAISING."
THE TIMES BOOK OF THE WEEK

"A GRIPPING MURDER MYSTERY"
SUNDAY EXPRESS

"DRIPPING WITH ATMOSPHERE AND GOTHIC GORE,
WILD BOY WILL APPEAL TO FANS OF SHERLOCK
HOLMES, GOTHIC HORROR AND ALL THINGS
MURDEROUS AND MYSTERIOUS."
JULIA ECCLESHARE, LOVEREADING4KIDS.CO.UK

"FREAK SHOWS, MYSTERIES AND INTRIGUE,
WHAT'S NOT TO LOVE? A BRILLIANTLY IMAGINED
HISTORICAL ADVENTURE."
TBK MAG

"HIS EVENTFUL LIFE WILL MESMERISE
BOYS IN PARTICULAR."
THE TIMES

"MIXING MYSTERY WITH ACTION, ADVENTURE
AND HISTORY AND THE CREEPY BACKDROP
OF THE FAIRGROUND, THIS BOOK WILL HOOK
YOUNG READERS FROM THE FIRST PAGE."
WE LOVE THIS BOOK

"A PLEASINGLY PACEY AND
ATMOSPHERIC HISTORICAL ROMP."
BOOKTRUST

WILD BOY

Rob LLOYD JONES

WALKER
BOOKS

THANK YOU

Huge thanks to everyone at Walker for making me feel
so welcome, especially Mara, Lucy, Gill and David, as well
as Deb at Candlewick Press. They all did magic.
Thanks to my amazing agent, Jo Unwin, without whose
early advice this book would not exist, to the brilliant team at
Conville & Walsh, and to Carol for helping me find the time.
Most importantly, thanks for a million reasons to
Mum, Dad, Sally and Otis. Love you all.

First published in Great Britain 2013 by Walker Books Ltd
87 Vauxhall Walk, London SE11 5HJ

This edition published 2014

2 4 6 8 10 9 7 5 3

Text © 2013 by Rob Lloyd Jones
Cover illustration © 2014 by Rui Ricardo
Interior illustrations © 2013 by Owen Davey

The right of Rob Lloyd Jones to be identified as author
and Rui Ricardo and Owen Davey as illustrators of this work has been asserted
by them in accordance with the Copyright, Designs and Patents Act 1988

This book has been typeset in Book Antiqua

Printed and bound in Great Britain by Clays Ltd, St Ives plc

British Library Cataloguing in Publication Data:
a catalogue record for this book is available from the British Library

ISBN 978-1-4063-6196-4

www.walker.co.uk

For Sally, for everything

PROLOGUE

SOUTHWARK, LONDON, MAY 1838

That night, the night the showman came, the moon was the colour of mud.

Above the houses the sky turned from black to dingy brown as a thick fog crept over the city. The monstrous mud-brown cloud rose from the river. It slithered over rooftops, curled around gas lamps and smothered their lights to ghostly orange globes. It crawled along the riverbank, swallowing the warehouses, workhouses and tumbledown tarry-black houses that leaned over the dark water. Doors were bolted. Shutters slammed. Even the rats in the alleys froze in fright as the cloud came rolling in. The fog swallowed everything – but not the showman.

His gloved fist banged on the workhouse door.

No reply.

He banged again.

There came a clunk, a thunk. A hatch in the door slid open and bloodshot eyes glared through. "Who the devil are you?" demanded a voice.

"I'm here for the boy," said the showman.

The eyes in the hatch narrowed. "What boy? There are *dozens* of boys."

The showman leaned forward, revealing his face in the shadow of his crooked top hat. It was a terrible face, ridged with so many scars he looked like he'd been sewn together from patches of skin. There were whip marks, knife cuts and scratches from nails. There were bite marks and burn marks and cuts from a saw. One long gash ran like purple warpaint over his bony nose. He stroked it with a finger as he leaned to the hatch and spoke in a growl.

"*The* boy," he said.

The bloodshot eyes widened. "Oh! *The* boy. One moment…"

Another thunk. Another clunk. The door swung open, revealing the owner of the bloodshot eyes – a plump, greasy individual who had been in the process of devouring a roast chicken. He wore the bird like a glove puppet, one hand inserted into its neck cavity so he could bite chunks from whichever part he pleased. Nibbling on a scab of skin, he eyed the showman warily.

"My name's Bledlow," he said. "I'm the master of this place."

The showman didn't reply.

The Master swallowed the skin. "You got the money?"

"Not till I seen the boy."

Composing himself, Master Bledlow unhooked an oil lamp from the wall. "Follow me," he said.

He led the way down a dark and dingy corridor. Cockroaches scurried into cracks. Damp glistened on bare walls. In a hall, a dozen boys in ragged gowns sat slurping bowls of gruel. One of the boys saw the showman, and grinned wolfishly. "He's here to see the monster!" he whispered.

"*Mon-ster!*" the others chimed. "*Mon-ster! Mon-ster!*"

With a flick of his arm, Bledlow sent his chicken carcass flying into the hall. Several boys pounced on it, snarling at one another.

"*Mon-ster! Mon-ster!*" the others chanted.

The Master raised his light, and led the showman up a rickety flight of stairs. At the top was a wooden door with a warning scratched in charcoal. *WILD ANIMAL! BEWARE!*

The Master glanced at the showman. "We keep him in here. On account of the fighting."

"Fighting?"

"Because of how he looks."

The door opened with a groan, and they stepped inside. The room was musty and dusty and stank of damp. A ragged crow was perched in a narrow window, its eyes gleaming like black diamonds in the lamplight. Beside the window, another animal nested among a bundle of sacks.

No, not an animal. It was a boy.

The boy sat very still, staring out of the window.

"That him?" the showman asked.

Master Bledlow raised his lamp so its light fell on the boy's back. "See?" he said.

And now the showman saw.

The boy was covered almost completely in hair. Dark brown hair, matted and tangled with dirt. It grew all over his back, his shoulders and his chest. A darker swathe hung from his head, and a thick layer spread all over his face, smoothed and parted down the middle. It hid the boy's features completely, apart from two big eyes, big like an owl's eyes. Startlingly green, they sparkled even in the murky light from the moon. As the boy sat perfectly still, those eyes moved at incredible speed, watching the foggy scene outside.

"Boy!" the Master said.

The boy didn't turn, didn't even flinch.

The Master reached towards him. "Stand up, boy!"

The boy slid away. "Beat me again, Bledlow," he said in a soft, parched voice, "and I'll set fire to your coat."

The Master snatched back his hand. He giggled nervously. "Beat you! What talk! This is a charitable institution... Stand up, will you!"

The boy rose. He wore a sack over his shoulders, and breeches that were so worn they looked like cobwebs around his thin, hairy legs. Beneath the sack and breeches, the dirty brown hair extended all over his short, slight frame.

"Will he do?" said the Master.

The scars across the showman's face pulsed. He tossed Bledlow a pouch of coins. "He got kin?" he said.

"Kin?"

"Family what might want him back?"

"Ha! Whatever family this boy had dumped him on my doorstep eight years ago. Ugly little baby too. Thought he was a drowned rat!"

"What about a name?"

"Never gave him one. What's the point? Some of the boys had a few suggestions though. Just for fun... How about Hairy Harold the Human Doormat? Or Billy the Baboon Boy? Wait, this is my favourite – The Wolf That Ate Red Riding—"

"Wild Boy," said the showman.

For the first time, the boy turned. His emerald eyes considered the showman, and he repeated the name softly. "Wild Boy..."

"You must be wondering who I am?" the showman said.

It was not a question that expected an answer. But now the boy's big eyes began to move again, taking in every inch of the showman – his boots, his top hat and each scar on his shattered face. It was almost as if he'd fallen into a trance, so fast did his eyes move, so still was his head.

The boy blinked. "You're a showman in a travelling fair," he said.

"Boy!" the Master snapped.

But the boy's eyes remained on the showman. "You were born somewhere near the coast, with a birthmark covering half your face. Your dad beat you for it with a belt and a chain, so you ran off to the navy."

"Boy!"

"But you were kicked out and whipped, probably for stealing. Since then you been in two gaols, seven knife fights, been garrotted twice and had half your ear bitten off by a—"

"Shut up, boy!"

The Master swung his lantern, striking the boy hard in the face. There was a burst of sparks, and the room plunged into darkness.

A coil of smoke drifted through the dark, tinged with the scent of burnt hair. And then – *scritch, scratch* – the lantern flint struck. A streak of light broke the dark.

The showman felt the stub of his missing earlobe. For the first time his cold eyes thawed. He looked uncertain. Scared, even. "How the hell did he know all that?" he said.

The Master gave another nervous laugh. "I ...

uh … I'm not sure. The other boys won't even speak to him. They think it's devilry."

The light grew brighter.

"I'll show him devilry," the showman said. "Gimme that light."

"Light? I haven't got the light."

The Master looked down, and screamed. His coat was on fire! He sprung back, bashing himself against the wall to put out the flames. "He set fire to my coat!" he squealed. "He *actually* set fire to my coat!"

In the corner, the boy burst into a wheezy laugh of triumph and delight. His green eyes twinkled and he clutched his stomach from laughing so hard. "I told you!" he said. "You mean old goat! I told you I'd—"

And then – *whump!* – the showman kicked the boy hard in the chest. It wasn't a mere whack like he'd had from the Master's lantern – it was a brutal, rib-breaking blow. Even the Master stopped flapping and stared, shocked by the savagery of the attack.

The boy slumped to the floor. He curled up, gasping.

The showman leaned down and grasped the boy's long hair. "You don't know one thing," he spat. "My name. It's Augustus T. Finch, and they call me the Carnival King. Know why? Cos I show the most revolting freaks at the fair. And I reckon you might be the most revoltingest I seen yet. So here's my offer… Don't pass out, boy! Look at me!"

The showman tugged the hair harder.

The boy's eyes rolled. Blood glistened on his lips.

"Here's my offer," the showman said. "*Absolutely nothing*. No pay, no holiday and sure as blazes no treatment as generous as you've had from this here Master. All you'll get is food, a roof and work. Times you'll wish like you was dead. Others you'll feel like you was. You'll get spat at, beat up plenty. One freak I showed got stabbed just for looking at a feller the wrong way. Joke of it was he had no eyes. So that's my offer. Take it or leave it."

Tears soaked into the hair on the boy's cheeks. But he gritted his teeth and fought back the pain in his chest. "Will I see things?" he whispered.

The showman glanced at Master Bledlow, puzzled by the question.

"He likes to watch things," Bledlow explained. "That's all the little runt does. Just sits there staring out that window."

The showman released the boy's hair, letting him fall back to the floor. "You'll see plenty, all right," he told him. "Only, where you're going, ain't much of it gonna be pretty."

"A freak show?" the boy asked.

"A freak show," the showman said.

"Listen to him, boy," spluttered Master Bledlow. "It's the only work something like you could ever hope to find."

Slowly, painfully, the boy rose. His legs buckled,

but he clutched the wall for support. Through a veil of hair, he looked the showman hard in the eye. "When do we leave?"

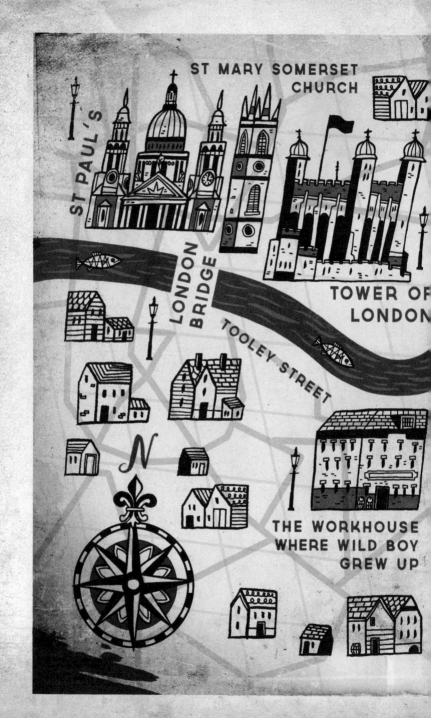

LONDON 1841

England

the THAMES

DOCKYARDS

GREENWICH PARK

PART 1

The Savage Spectacle
OF WILD BOY

1

GREENWICH, LONDON, OCTOBER 1841

It had rained for two days straight and Greenwich Fair was a washout. The showmen had lined the path through the fairground with straw, but the mud seeped through, forming a squelchy bog underfoot. At least the weather had finally cleared. Steamboats jostled at Greenwich Pier, packed lifeboat-tight with boozy revellers looking to make up for lost time. Drunken crowds streamed through the park gates, whooping and cheering, leaping on shoulders, shrieking like monkeys.

All along the path, showmen laid tables and hung banners, frantic to catch the last of the day's trade. There were peep shows, puppet shows, conjurers and card sharps. There were coconut shies, roundabouts, mesmerists and magicians. Ventriloquists argued with evil-eyed dolls, and wine-nosed Punch squawked *"That's the way to do it"* as he thrashed his wife with a policeman's stick.

Between the drinking booths and the circus tent sat a dismal line of wooden caravans that were peeling with paint and propped up with poles. Garish banners hung across their sides, painted with fantastically impossible scenes – a mermaid combing her hair, a giant towering over a lighthouse, a sheep with six legs, smoking a pipe. One of the signs read *CABINET OF CURIOSITIES*. Another said *EXHIBITION OF ODDITIES*. But most people called these vans freak shows. Top-hatted showmen leaned from their doors, speckling the air with spit as they called to the passing crowds.

"Have you seen Bradley Sirkis? He's a man with three eyes and no nose."

"She transforms from beauty to beast in front of your eyes."

"She walks, she talks, she wiggles, she giggles."

"He hops on the spot like a frog."

"World's largest!"

"World's smallest!"

"The greatest curiosity in the world!"

Drunken eyes gazed at the banners. No one saw the small figure on top of one of the vans, or the wide green eyes that watched from above...

Wild Boy lay still on the caravan roof, his heart hammering against the wooden boards. From up here he could see all the way along the path that cut through the fairground, from the park gates to the circus tent, and all the stalls and shows between. His eyes moved with incredible speed, picking out details from the bustling scene. He saw a lipstick smudge on a starched collar. He saw marks from prison irons on a wrist. A speck of paint on a stovepipe hat. A flare in a cardsharp's nostrils that said the man was cheating. A bulge in a lady's bonnet where something stolen was stashed. A girl playing leapfrog who —

Just then, the girl looked up and saw him.

Wild Boy flinched back, ready to dive through the hatch in the van roof if the girl screamed. But the girl *didn't* scream. Instead, a smile rose across her spotty cheeks.

The hairs tingled all over Wild Boy's body. Was she smiling at *him*? He shifted up and, very slowly, raised a hand in reply. But now the girl's mouth curled into a malicious grin. She pointed at him and shrieked to her friends, "Look! Monster! Monster! I seen a hairy monster!"

Wild Boy dropped to the roof, cursing himself. Of course she wasn't smiling at him!

In a puddle on the roof, he looked at his reflection. The girl was right, he *was* a monster. Only monsters looked like this – with dark, dirty hair all over his face, other than a thin line where it parted down the middle. The hair covered his hands too, and almost every part of his body. Thick clumps of it sprung from the sleeves of his coat, like a scarecrow bursting with straw.

"Wild Boy! Wild Boy!" a voice cried. "Hear what they say about Wild Boy! He's the missing link between man and bear!"

Below, the showman Augustus Finch stood on the caravan steps. The scars across his face throbbed as he waggled a hand at the banner on the van – a lurid painting of a boy with glowing eyes and shredded clothes transforming into some sort of wild animal.

"Wild Boy! Wild Boy! Hear what they say about Wild Boy! He's wild! He's wonderful! He's one of a kind! This way, ladies and gentlemen! You won't see a more revolting freak at this fairground or any other, or your penny back – guaranteed!"

Wild Boy sighed. That was his cue.

As he turned to the hatch in the roof, he looked again down the path. The gang of girls had gone, laughing and leapfrogging towards the circus. Then, as he watched, the girl who had screamed at him tripped and fell face-forward into the mud.

A grin spread across Wild Boy's hairy face, and the sparkle returned to his eyes. "Good," he said.

He swung through the hatch and into the van. It was show time.

2

The caravan air was thick with the stench of sweat and rotting wood.

Wild Boy hung by hairy fingertips from the hatch in the roof, his bare feet groping for the ladder on the wall. Not finding it, he let go and landed with a *thud* that shuddered the van and made the ceiling lamp sway on its hook.

"Caught you!" a voice said.

Wild Boy whirled around, fearing it was Finch. But it was just the showman's assistant, Sir Oswald Farley.

"Master Wild," Sir Oswald said. "Mr Finch would not be pleased were he to catch you sneaking around outside."

Wild Boy grinned. He'd lived with Sir Oswald for three years but still found it funny to hear his posh voice. "The old goat's gotta catch me first," he said.

Sir Oswald muttered something disapproving as he helped Wild Boy up with one hand, his other pressed hard against the floor. Sir Oswald had no legs. Instead he got about on his hands, which were as tough and leathery as his wrinkled old face. But, despite his disability, he always looked immaculate in his tailcoat, top hat and tie. There wasn't a speck of dirt on his face, a rare achievement in a place as filthy as a travelling fair.

"I wish you would not take such risks," he fussed.

It *was* a risk, Wild Boy knew – Augustus Finch didn't allow him to go outside between shows. But it was worth it. The less time he spent in this van, the better. He didn't mind the smell or the constant cold, or even the rainwater that leaked through worm-holes in the roof. It was the stage that he hated – the upturned crates, and the tatty red cloth for a curtain. Propped beside them against the wall was a rusty camp bed with a strip of cloth hung between its legs. Its painted slogan read *DEEP IN THE JUNGLE TERROR AWAITS!*

Sir Oswald rushed to the stage, his strong upper body swinging between his hands as his coat-tails dragged behind him along the floor. He hoisted himself onto the crates, and hid behind the curtain. "Quickly, Master Wild," he said.

Wild Boy hesitated, glancing up at the hatch in the roof. He wished that he could climb back out-side and hide there all day, watching the crowds.

He wished he could do anything other than this, the sort of things that normal people did. It was the same dream he had before every show, but he knew it was just a cruel fantasy. He wasn't normal, he was a freak. This was where he belonged.

"Just get on with it," he whispered.

He rushed to the stage and joined Sir Oswald behind the curtain.

Getting ready didn't take long. Apart from his breeches, Wild Boy wore only one item of clothing – a long, red drummer-boy's coat with gold tassels, which he'd stolen from a marching band last year. For the show, he simply unbuttoned it so the audience could see more of the hair all over his body.

"Master Wild!" Sir Oswald said. "Look at this hair! Such a state. All this dirt and mud… And is that horse dung? Don't you ever wash?"

It *was* horse dung, Wild Boy knew, and he never washed. Partly because there wasn't much opportunity – clean water was rare at most sites where the travelling fair pitched. But, more than that, he didn't think there was much point.

"Why bother?" he said.

"Why bother? Manners for a start, young man."

"Monsters don't have manners," Wild Boy said, with a grin.

"Monsters indeed," Sir Oswald said, brushing the long, tangled hair on Wild Boy's chest.

Wild Boy stepped suddenly back. A bolt of anger

shot through him, and his hands curled into fists. "Don't touch me!" he snapped.

Sir Oswald slid away, staring at the marks he'd seen on the pallid skin beneath Wild Boy's hair – old scars from the workhouse master's belt, and from all his fights there with the other boys.

Wild Boy messed his hair up again, hiding the marks. He hadn't meant to shout at Sir Oswald. He just didn't like being touched, and those scars were the reason. Dark memories came creeping from the place at the back of his mind, where he kept them hidden. But he forced them back again, and sniffed.

"They ain't nothing," he said.

Sir Oswald looked at him, the wrinkles on his face easing away. "Master Wild," he said softly, "I apologize."

"They ain't nothing, Sir Oswald. Besides, I'm a monster, remember?"

Sir Oswald smiled, although his eyes stayed sad. Wild Boy could tell that his friend wanted to ask more about the scars, and his past life in the workhouse. But he didn't want to talk about it. He *couldn't*.

Eager to change the subject, he forced a smile of his own, and stepped closer. "You say I ain't a monster, eh? How about this then…?"

Alarm flashed across Sir Oswald's face. "No, Master Wild! Don't—"

Grabbing him under the armpits, Wild Boy lifted him into the air. "Raaaa!" he joked. "I'm a savage monster! I'm half boy, half bear and half wolf an' all! I already ate your legs and now I'll have the rest of you!"

Sir Oswald wriggled in his grasp, trying to fight a grin. "Master Wild, if you do not unhand me this instant I shall be forced to clip your ear."

Wild Boy set him carefully back on the stage. He knew that Sir Oswald wasn't really angry. His friend understood what it was like to look different to other people. Years ago Sir Oswald had been the star of Finch's freak show. Billed as "Little Lord Handyman," he'd performed tricks on his hands as he told stories of how he'd lost his legs at the Battle of Waterloo. But since then people had lost their appetite for heroes. Now they had a taste for monsters.

Sir Oswald looked through a hole in the stage curtain. "Here they come," he warned.

The caravan door opened and Augustus Finch led an audience inside. The showman moved among them, listening to their coins clink into his tin. Six clinks. Finch's face cracked into a satisfied sneer. He slicked back his greasy black and white hair to show off his collection of scars.

"Ladies and gentlemen," he began. "The tale I'm about to tell is truly shocking…"

No, it ain't, Wild Boy thought. The only shocking thing was how long Finch had been telling it. The showman gave the same patter before every show, a tale about the "creature Wild Boy", who was raised in a forest by bears. But Wild Boy didn't mind the story – after all, it sounded a nicer way to grow up than in his old workhouse. And besides, it gave him a few minutes to spy on the audience.

He peered through the curtain hole, his sharp eyes taking in every detail.

"Do you see anything interesting?" Sir Oswald whispered.

"Don't see nothing," Wild Boy said.

"Poppycock! You see *everything*, Master Wild."

Although he pretended not to understand, Wild Boy knew he did see things differently to others. All those hours he'd spent staring through his workhouse window, searching for clues to the world outside, the world he dreamed of being part of. From tiny details on people's faces and clothes, he'd learned to paint whole pictures of their lives. It had become instinctive. He read people like code.

Not that there was much to see about this mob. Steam rose from their thick coats, and even from behind the curtain he could smell the booze on their breath. One man had bruised knuckles. One woman had sick on her chin. Except...

"*The priest*," Wild Boy whispered.

At the back of the audience was a priest. That wasn't unusual – priests often visited fairs to preach to people about their sins. Only, Wild Boy could tell immediately that this man was an impostor.

He closed his eyes and thought about the priests

he'd watched around the camps. Sometimes, when he remembered things, it was as if the images were frozen in his head. He could study them like they were paintings framed on a wall. He visualized one priest, then another. Both men had scuffs on their trouser knees from praying, and soot on their fingers from snuffing out candles. *This* man, though, had neither of these things. He *did* have a dog collar that looked like it was made of newspaper (specifically the *Morning Chronicle*), a Bible that had barely been opened, judging from the lack of wear on the spine, and a sheen of nervous sweat glistening above his upper lip.

What kind of man pretends to be a priest in a crowd? Wild Boy wondered.

The answer revealed itself a second later, when he saw the man's hand dip into a lady's shawl and – fast as a flash – remove a purse. He was a pickpocket!

"Positions, Master Wild!" Sir Oswald said as he hid behind the propped-up bed next to the stage. "Here we go."

A crazy idea entered Wild Boy's head. He tried to push it away but it wormed its way back, growing fat with possibility. What if he saved one of these people from the thief? Would they thank him? Better still, would they take him away from this place, to a new life? Maybe… Maybe it wasn't such a fantasy.

"Master Wild?" Sir Oswald whispered. "Are you quite well? You are shaking."

Wild Boy turned, wide eyes staring at his friend. "Sir Oswald, do you think people like us could be anything else?"

"What do you mean?"

"I mean... Something other than freaks."

Sir Oswald slid from behind the bed, although his face remained hidden in shadow. He lowered his voice – Wild Boy had never heard him sound so serious. "Master Wild, I *do*. I do think that. But whatever makes you ask me this now?"

"I... It's nothing. You'd better hide."

Sir Oswald looked reluctant to abandon the conversation. But he heard the showman's speech coming to an end, and disappeared back behind the bed.

"Gather in close!" Finch cried. "Gather in and get a good gawp. Prepare yourselves for the most hideous, most revolting, most sickeningest sight in all of England. Ladies and gentlemen, I give you *The Savage Spectacle of Wild Boy!*"

With a flourish of his hand, the showman yanked away the curtain.

The act had been the same ever since Wild Boy joined the freak show, and they performed it up to twenty times a day at these larger fairs, so he knew it well. As the curtain fell he should have been snarling like a dog and chewing an old bone at the side of the stage. But this time, he just stood staring, lost in increasingly excited thoughts.

The crowd didn't care – they'd just come to see a

freak, and Wild Boy certainly fitted that description. The group huddled closer, their mouths puckered in delighted disgust.

"Ugly bugger," one of them said.

"Looks like a baby werewolf."

"Or a stinking armpit!"

Wild Boy tried not to listen. He heard the same jokes every day, and dozens much more cruel. At the workhouse, he'd always fought back against boys who teased him, which meant he'd got into a lot of fights. Eventually, he'd been locked up alone in that cell. When he'd joined the travelling show, he'd done the same – leaping from the stage, punching and spitting at anyone who yelled abuse. But these weren't boys in a workhouse. Here, the bullies were a lot tougher. Most nights during those first few months, Wild Boy hadn't been able to sleep from the pain of his bruises. He'd been lucky though – plenty of punters at fairs carried knives, clubs and even garrotting wires. It wouldn't have been long before he punched the wrong person.

So he'd made a new rule. As long as no one touched him, he'd put up with the teasing. This was a freak show, and he was a freak, after all. He hoped that, eventually, he'd become numb to the names, or not even hear them. But he still did. And, even after all this time, they still stung.

That afternoon, though, his attention was focused entirely on the thief as he watched the man swipe another purse and then a pocket watch from a fob. There was only one person he hadn't yet robbed, an old man at the front of the small group.

Wild Boy studied the man and, in seconds, knew that he was a retired soldier, an opium addict, was heavily in debt and that he had come to the fair to gamble the last of his pennies at the card tables. The clues were obvious enough: the red-brown tinge to the man's teeth caused by smoke from the opium pipe and the slight tremble of his hands from withdrawal were clear indications of the man's addiction. The sprig of heather in his pocket suggested that he'd visited one of the gypsies at the park gates, a sign of both desperation and concern for his immediate fortunes. And as for the man's military past and current debt problem, Wild Boy could see that he'd once worn medals on his coat – the darker patch on his lapel, unfaded by the sun, showed where they'd been displayed. But the pin holes didn't look torn, so the medals hadn't been ripped off by thieves. More likely they'd been sold, and only the most desperate of men would trade the trophies he'd once worn so proudly.

All of this was brilliant news to Wild Boy. Surely the man would be even more grateful than most, were he to have his last pennies saved from the fingers of a pickpocket. Wild Boy wondered if the man would give him a job. He'd happily work for free, as a servant. Maybe he could have a real name, something like a normal life. Eventually, perhaps the old gentleman would adopt him as a son, like in the plays they staged at some of the fairs…

By now Wild Boy was so excited that he forgot to breathe, and he coughed.

The old gentleman stepped back, closer to the thief's probing hand.

How could Wild Boy warn him? He had to be polite, he decided, to show the man that he wasn't a monster. He'd learned a few posh words from Sir Oswald that might do the trick. But he needed to act fast, before the pickpocket struck…

Now!

He jumped from the stage and landed with a *thump* beside the old man. "Good sir!" he said. "May I be so bold as to offer a word of—"

"MONSTER!"

The old man screamed in fright, stepped back and thrashed Wild Boy with his cane. Wild Boy reacted without thinking – first punching the man in the nose, and then shoving him back into the pick-pocket. "Don't you bloody touch me!" he yelled.

In a rush of panic he tried to scramble up onto the stage, but the old man grabbed his long hair and yanked him back. Wild Boy turned and lashed out again, swearing and whirling his fists. But now the others joined in against him too. A woman kicked his shin. Someone else punched his jaw.

"Get off me!" he cried. "There's a thief!"

"He says he's a thief!"

"Get him to the ground!"

"Bloody freaks!"

One of them stamped on Wild Boy's bare foot and he tumbled over. He curled up as they surrounded him, raining blows.

Augustus Finch hopped excitedly around the scene. "One penny for a kick!" he cried. "Pay up, pay up! Anyone that kicks him owes me a penny!"

And then they were gone, a crush of limbs squeezing through the door. The showman skipped behind them, calling to the punters who had gathered outside. "Hear what they say! Hear what they say about Wild Boy! He's wild! He's wonderful! You can kick him for a penny!"

Wild Boy rolled over, groaning and muttering obscenities. Every part of his body ached. But more than that, he felt angry. Not at the old gentleman, but at himself.

"Idiot…" he muttered. Then he yelled so loud that it shook the ceiling lamp on its hook. "BLOODY IDIOT FREAK!"

He lay on the floor, anger coursing through his veins. He wanted to scream even louder, to burst up and kick the caravan walls until he'd smashed this whole van into pieces. But he knew it would do no good. This was his life. If not this freak show then another one.

Sir Oswald appeared from behind the bed. "Whatever was that about, old chap?"

"Nothing," Wild Boy muttered. "Just a stupid idea."

They looked at each other for a moment, and he knew that Sir Oswald understood. His friend smiled at him sadly as he helped him up from the floor. "Come on," he said. "Better get ready for the next lot."

3

That night a wind rose across the camp, creaking the van like a ship in a storm. Wild Boy pulled his coat tighter around him and nestled in the bundle of sacks that formed his bed. Wherever the travelling fair pitched, the freak shows always closed by sundown. Even the most desperate showmen weren't prepared to spend all evening throwing out drunks and breaking up fights. Because at night the fairground turned savage.

Wild Boy knew the scenes well. Naphtha lights and oil lamps lit grinning, sweaty faces as drunken crowds danced through a haze of steam and tobacco smoke. Some people shrieked from behind carnival masks – black-feathered monsters, or eerie white faces with long, crooked noses. Others propped up booze stalls, swigging from pots of beer and pints of gin. The dancing booths rocked and pounded to the sound of violins while gangs of ruffians prowled the path, knocking off hats and shrieking, "Haw haw! Haw haw!"

Often Wild Boy sat for hours, watching it all through a crack in the wall. It was the only time he ever relaxed – forgetting about his own life and exploring those of others. He sometimes felt as if he was floating through the crack and in among the scenes outside, seeing everything...

But that night, he couldn't calm down. It wasn't just the fight in the show, it was this place too. Greenwich was not far from Southwark, and his old workhouse. The memories were still painful, of all those times that strangers had come to see him in his room. His heart had surged with the hope that they'd come to take him away to a different life, a normal life. But really, they'd just paid Master Bledlow to see the freak. And today he'd got carried away again in that same stupid fantasy. He should've known better by now. He'd never be anything other than the Savage Spectacle of Wild Boy.

He slid across the van and spied through another hole, hoping he'd see something to take his mind off things among the backstage jumble of prop carts and supply wagons that spread behind the path. Nearby, two other freak-show performers – the Human Colossus and the Living Skeleton – were fighting with tent pegs. The Oldest Woman in the World, the Bearded Lady and Mr Peculiar crowded around, goading them and gambling on the result.

Wild Boy's eyes widened as he watched the scene intently. His breaths grew deeper, rustling the hair on his cheeks…

"Hey, mutt! Ugly mutt!"

Augustus Finch sat on the edge of his camp bed, greasy black and white hair hanging down over his face. He picked mud from the hobnails on his boots and drank deeply from his third bottle of beer. Drinking was Finch's favourite activity. After dark it was his only activity.

"Get me another beer, mutt."

Wild Boy shoved a bottle into the showman's hand, fighting the urge to throw it at his face. He glanced up at the deep red birthmark that stained the cheek beneath the showman's scars. The mark, Wild Boy knew, was why Finch's father had beaten him – because his son had looked different to other people.

"What are you gawping at?" Finch snarled. The showman put a hand against his cheek. "I said, what are you looking at, mutt?"

"Nothing," Wild Boy said. "Ain't looking at nothing."

The door opened and a sack of firewood thumped into the entrance. Sir Oswald followed it, pulling his legless body up the steps and into the van. "Evening, all," he puffed.

Wild Boy rushed to help, although Sir Oswald's

arms were so strong he had no trouble lifting the sack. The man spent half of his life fixing up this van, screwing springs to the axles or bolting pipes to the walls. Beneath the banners, the wooden walls were criss-crossed with tubes, like the scars on Finch's face.

"Extraordinary ventilation!" Sir Oswald often explained. "Incredible new heating system! Wait until you feel the suspension, Master Wild. You will think we are gliding over ice!"

As far as Wild Boy could tell, none of the repairs had made any difference – the van was still cold, it still stank and it rattled terribly as they travelled over country roads between the fairs. Rather, he thought that Sir Oswald kept working simply because he *had* to. Like him, he had no other place to go.

That was just a guess, though. Wild Boy had a harder time reading Sir Oswald than he did anyone else at the fair. His friend had streaks of grey in his hair, and wrinkles on his face, but he moved as fast on his hands as any young man on his feet. He called himself *Sir* Oswald, but Wild Boy had no idea if the title was real. He kept an old clothes chest in his corner of the van, but he didn't store much in it. So eventually, Wild Boy gave up searching for clues. He was just happy that Sir Oswald was his friend, the first and only friend he'd ever had.

"Watching the fight, eh?" Sir Oswald said. He peered through the crack in the wood. "The Colossus versus the Skeleton? Not much of a contest there. Used to box a little myself you know, back when I had pins. Mind you, never against a brute the size of the Colossus."

"The Living Skeleton will win," Wild Boy said.

"Poppycock! The man is so thin I can count his ribs through his vest."

"He was in the army."

"I have never heard him say that."

Wild Boy doubted that anyone had. Few of the freaks spoke of their past. Some found it too depressing to speak of happier times. Others, like him, simply had no happier times to speak of.

Sir Oswald leaned closer to the crack, studying the Skeleton curiously. "Master Wild, how could you possibly know that he was in the army?"

"See the white bits of his eyes?" Wild Boy said.

"Barely!"

"They got black specks in them. They're powder burns from musket fire. You see the same on soldiers about the fair."

"Perhaps *you* do, Master Wild…"

"And look how he folded his coat, and that old tattoo on his arm. Army bloke, no doubt about it. Watch this now…"

Outside, the Living Skeleton swung a fist. The Human Colossus fell to the mud with a splash and a mighty thump.

"Outstanding!" Sir Oswald said. "Master Wild,

you do have an extraordinary skill."

"Ain't no skill," Wild Boy said. "It's just looking."

"Poppycock."

Wild Boy shrugged. It was just what came from years of being locked up with nothing to do but watch the world and dream that he was someone else. It wasn't just his eyes that were sharp either. Confined to that room, he'd learned to separate individual sounds from the roar of the city – the barks of different dogs, or the rattle of particular carriages. He could distinguish between hundreds of smells, and had taught himself to read just from posters and placards he'd seen through the window. He didn't see any of it as being particularly skilful. It was just what came from being a freak.

"Right," Sir Oswald said, "I shall test you." He moved across the van and looked through another crack. "How about that lady there? What can you tell me about her?"

Wild Boy didn't like talking about the way he saw things. He knew that it was something different about him, and he hated being different. But he couldn't help himself. It was too much fun. He joined Sir Oswald and peered eagerly out onto the path.

"Which lady?" he asked.

"The one in the green bonnet."

"She's a seamstress in a factory."

"Now how could you know that?"

"She has blisters on the insides of her fingers,

probably from the needles. And her old bonnet's fixed up with different coloured threads, see? Most likely, scraps from her factory, otherwise why not buy the right colour?"

"Incredible! And how about that man in the smock?"

"He's a boxer. Lost his last fight for money."

"Scoundrel!"

"He needed it for his new baby, a boy."

"Ah well, that's fair game. And that woman there?"

"She's a flower seller."

"Now how could you *possibly* know that?"

"Cos she's selling flowers."

They slid back from the wall, both laughing. Wild Boy felt a warm glow inside. He realized that he was proud to have impressed Sir Oswald.

"What are you two snickering at?" said Augustus Finch. The showman, half asleep and fully drunk, sat up on his bed. Again he covered the birthmark on his cheek. "You're laughing at me, ain't you?"

He hurled a bottle across the caravan. It smashed against the wall, showering Sir Oswald with beer and broken glass.

"Hey!" Wild Boy yelled. He grabbed a bottle to throw back, but Sir Oswald grasped his arm.

"Don't, Master Wild."

Wild Boy knew he was right – picking a fight with Finch was a bad idea. Over the past few years, he'd seen the showman gouge eyes, bite off noses, even cut off a man's tongue up in Liverpool. But the anger that often overwhelmed Wild Boy had returned, like a drum beating inside him. He couldn't calm down.

"Clean up that mess," Finch said as he slumped back on his bed. "And get me another drink."

Sir Oswald's hand tightened on Wild Boy's arm. A sad smile spread across his leathery face. "Things will get better, Master Wild. You will see."

Wild Boy tried to return the smile, but it wouldn't come. He wondered how his friend always remained so hopeful. Sir Oswald had performed in a freak show. He'd suffered the same abuse. But still, he really believed that life would get better for people who looked different.

"Here you are, Mr Finch," Sir Oswald said, placing the beer bottle in the showman's hand.

"Clean that up an' all, runt," Finch said.

Sir Oswald slid back, revolted by the sight of the showman's chamber pot on the floor. The reeking bowl was filled with sloppy brown excrement.

Finch's face cracked into a sneer. "Get it nice and sparkling, like."

Wild Boy's fists clenched into hairy balls. *Stay calm*, he urged himself. But his hands shook with anger. Before he could stop himself he sprang up and yelled at Finch across the van. "Clean that up yourself, you old goat!"

The showman bolted up. "*What* did you just say to me?"

"Nothing!" Sir Oswald said. "He didn't say anything! Here, I shall clean it up..."

"Don't do it!" Wild Boy insisted. "He can bloomin' do it himself."

Slowly, Augustus Finch rose. "Say that again, mutt."

Wild Boy knew what would happen now. It was the same whenever he stood up to Finch, or to Master Bledlow back when he'd lived at the workhouse. Now he was going to get badly hurt. But he wouldn't back down, even though he felt physically sick with fear. He wouldn't give Finch the satisfaction.

He tried to sound brave, but his voice betrayed him and he couldn't stop it from cracking. "It... It just ain't right," he said.

Before he could react, the showman struck him across the face, and then kicked him hard in the chest. Wild Boy tumbled back and crashed against the caravan stove in a burst of sparks.

Finch towered over him. "Cry!" he roared. "I wanna hear you cry for once, you disgusting, ugly mutt!"

The sharp taste of blood stung Wild Boy's mouth, and his chest screamed where the showman's hobnail boot had hit him. Part of him wanted to curl up and beg Finch for forgiveness, because then the showman would leave him alone. But he wouldn't – he *couldn't*.

He pressed a hand against the wall and rose unsteadily to his feet. He'd put up a fight, that much he *could* do. Maybe he could even add a new scar to Finch's collection, before the showman beat him unconscious. That would be something, at least.

He hocked up a ball of spit and blood, and fired it to the floor beside the showman's boots. "I ain't crying for no one," he said.

He expected another attack, but now Finch turned to Sir Oswald. The showman's eyes gleamed with ferocity. "And *you*..."

Sir Oswald tried to crawl away, but Finch dragged him back and thrust his face at the chamber pot. "You can *lick* that up now, runt!"

Wild Boy knew he should leave. He could sleep in the stable hut, come back tomorrow. But something inside him had snapped. He'd had enough.

He reached down and picked up a shard of the broken beer bottle. "You let him go, Finch."

Finch snorted. He released Sir Oswald and stepped closer to Wild Boy. "You got some nerve, boy, I'll give you that. You say you won't cry? Ha! Before I'm done with you, you're gonna scream like a baby."

The showman struck out, but this time Wild Boy was ready. Ducking Finch's arm, he dropped to the floor and rammed the glass dagger into the showman's boot. A savage roar came from his mouth, rage at three years of cruel treatment as he felt the weapon tear through leather and into flesh.

Finch gave a blood-curdling scream. He tumbled back and landed on the chamber pot, a wave of foul brown filth washing over his head.

Before the showman could get up, Wild Boy leaped on him and hit him with the pot. "That's for picking on Sir Oswald!" he yelled. "And this is for everything else!"

He whacked Finch again, then again, harder. With each strike, his panic mounted, and more tears filled his eyes. He knew he had to run. He had nowhere to go, but he *had* to run. Dropping the pot, he jumped over the showman and burst through the door. Sir Oswald cried out for him to stop, but he was already gone. His long coat swished red and gold as he fled the freak show and into the fair.

4

"**B**oy! Where are you, boy? I'll wring your ugly neck!"

Wild Boy lay flat on one of the caravan roofs. His heart pounded so hard he was sure it would give him away. He didn't move, didn't even breathe.

Below, Augustus Finch stalked along the back of the vans. The web of scars flushed across the showman's face, and a glob of spit hung like a spider from his chin. He limped painfully from the cut on his foot. The glass shard that had inflicted the wound was gripped in his hand, ready to use in revenge.

"You'll be back!" he screamed. "You hear me, you ugly mutt? You'll be back, cos where else has a freak like you got to go? But you won't need to worry about your hair no more. Cos I'm gonna skin you alive!"

Wild Boy's face burned with anger. He wanted

to leap from the van and smash the showman to the ground. But this time he fought back the rage. He'd been lucky against Finch in the van, and knew that only a fool would challenge him twice in one night.

So he lay still, as rainwater from the roof seeped through his coat and soaked the hair on his chest. He lay still until the showman was gone and his cries were drowned by the roar of the fair.

Even then Wild Boy didn't move. He was trying not to cry. He'd spent his whole life not crying, no matter how badly he'd been treated or teased. But he was so scared right then. He'd never seen Finch that angry. If he went back, the showman would beat him to within an inch of his life, and he wouldn't care that the star of his show couldn't perform for a week.

He pulled his coat tighter as an icy wind swept over the rooftops. He knew that he had to go back – what else could he do? Certainly nothing normal; a freak show was the only life someone like him was good for. One or two freaks had got away to run their own shows, but first they'd saved up money to rent a van and horse. Wild Boy hadn't earned a single penny during his time with Finch.

Unless…

Unless he could *steal* some money. How hard could it be? He just had to find the right target, someone who wouldn't miss a few pennies from their pocket.

He slid to the edge of the roof, his sharp eyes raking the crowds. From here he could see all the way to the circus tent at the end of the path, a swirl of colour against the soot-black sky. There were hundreds of people down there. He saw a beggar with a sign saying *SHIPWRECKED SAILOR* (whom he could tell had never been to sea). He saw four women playing cards (three of whom he knew were cheating). He saw a woman faking a fit outside a gin tent, a man with a hook for a hand, a girl stealing gingerbread...

His eyes landed on a wealthy-looking couple buying chestnuts for their daughter. Was there something to steal there? No, they only *looked* wealthy. The mother's ears were pierced but she wasn't wearing earrings even though the family was all dressed up. The girl's expensive dress was patched in three places, and two of the father's mother-of-pearl shirt buttons were missing – pawned, Wild Boy guessed, to provide for his family.

No – he couldn't steal from them.

Suddenly he sat up. Across the path, a dark figure moved between the vans. Someone was shadowing the family – stopping when they stopped, moving when they moved, darting from behind one van to the next.

Another thief, Wild Boy realized.

He wasn't surprised. The family was an obvious target. They didn't just look rich, they looked scared too. Wild Boy watched as they made their way cautiously along the side of the path, as far as possible from the threatening crowds. Soon they would brush past a banner for the circus. That, he guessed, was where the thief would strike. And he had a good idea who that thief was too…

He turned away, trying to forget what he'd seen. "Ain't none of my business," he muttered.

Only… That family wasn't rich, but they were going to get robbed unless he did something about it. He imagined how they would feel when they discovered they'd lost what little money they had.

He cursed, banged a palm against the rooftop. He would warn them, that was all. He'd give them a flash of his face – that was enough to scare anyone off.

A moment later he was running again behind the vans. His long coat fluttered as he leaped over planks supporting sinking wheels, and weaved between guy ropes where showmen had pitched tents backstage. He ran right around the circus tent and to the backs of the caravans on the other side of the path. He ducked down an alley between two of the vans and finally stopped, catching his breath. A strip of cloth hung across the other end of the alley, painted with a slogan for the circus. *MRS EVERETT'S MOST MARVELLOUS SHOW!*

Wild Boy felt a glow of satisfaction. He'd got there before the thief.

He crept to the end of the alley and peeled back the banner. Yards away, dozens of people trudged along the path. He was relieved to see that the family didn't need help after all – they had already turned back towards the park gates, moving so fast they were almost running. Wild Boy watched them go for a moment. The girl was crying, but how he envied the life that she was running back to. He hoped for her sake that she could forget all about this terrible place.

Just then something dropped from the top of a van and landed with a *splash* behind Wild Boy in the mud. It was the thief!

He whirled around but the person was too fast, a blur of red and gold. A fist punched him in the stomach. A boot kicked him hard in the shin.

"I saw you, freak," said a voice. "You scared off my mark."

Before Wild Boy could react, the thief leaped over him in a single acrobatic bound. He turned to fight, but again he was too slow, and the thief booted him painfully in the backside. He staggered forward. His head whacked against the caravan wall, and he tumbled into the mud.

The boots squelched closer. "And now you're going to pay."

5

Wild Boy looked up through a veil of wet and tangled hair.

The face of a girl glared down at him, as pale as the moon except for strawberry freckles that dotted her cheeks. Her long hair was the colour of rust, and her dress was covered in red and gold sequins that shimmered in the moonlight.

Wild Boy scrabbled back between the vans, his heart pounding. This was Clarissa Everett, a teenage acrobat from the circus. He'd been enemies with her since the day he joined the fair. That day, more than ever, he had needed to show people that, although he might be small, he'd fight anyone who laid a finger on him. Clarissa had been the first to try, and he'd smashed one of her teeth with a stick. None of the other fairground children had picked on him since.

Clarissa stood over him, fists bunched and freckles flared. "This end of the path is circus territory," she said. "Freaks don't belong here, nor rats neither. And you're both."

Gripping the caravan wheel, Wild Boy pulled himself up. He guessed that Clarissa was only a year older than him, and almost as slim, but she was tough too – an acrobat by day and a fairground thief by night. He had to show her he was tougher.

He brushed long hair from his eyes, hocked up a ball of spit and fired it to the ground between them. "Fight then," he said.

Clarissa did the same, her spit landing inches from his bare feet. "Fight," she agreed.

"To the death," Wild Boy added, holding her glare.

Clarissa hesitated. "What?"

"If we fight, it's to the death. Them's the rules."

"I ain't fighting to the death! I'm just going to kick your teeth out. I followed that family all the way from the gates until you scared 'em off. They were rich toffs."

"Ha! All you'd have got was an empty pocket book. They weren't toffs. At least not no more."

"How could *you* know that?"

"I saw."

"Saw?"

Wild Boy cursed. Other than Sir Oswald, he didn't tell anyone about the way he saw things, and especially not Clarissa. But he sensed an opportunity to make some money, so he wouldn't have to go back to Finch.

"How about this?" he said. "I'll find you another toff, a real one this time, for half of what you steal."

"I don't need help from a *freak*."

"Then we gotta fight," Wild Boy said.

"I don't need to fight you neither. I already won." She flicked her hair from her eyes, and turned to look past the banner. "Go back to your monster museum," she said.

Wild Boy considered giving her a kick. But he knew this wasn't over yet. He needed Clarissa's help, but she needed him too. "Fair enough," he said as coolly as he could. "Find a toff yourself then."

He turned to walk away.

"Wait," Clarissa said. "How can *you* find one?"

Got her, Wild Boy thought. But he tried not to smile. "Always a couple of rich types about," he said. "They come in disguise so they won't get robbed."

"Nonsense. Who?"

"Fifty-fifty, even split." He spat on his palm to shake on the deal.

"I'm not touching your spit! If you do find a toff, I *might* give you some of the takings."

There was no use arguing. Better to see what she stole, Wild Boy thought, and then decide if it was worth fighting for. He moved closer.

"Don't you dare touch me," Clarissa warned. "I don't wanna catch nothing."

But Wild Boy barely heard. Already his eyes were searching the crowd, homing in on tiny, telling details that flashed past the banner. Only after a minute or so did he notice that Clarissa was staring at the hair on his face. He turned, and she looked back to the path.

"So?" she said. "Where's this toff then?"

"There. That man in the cloak."

Clarissa gave a derisive snort. The man Wild Boy had selected was young and handsome, with bushy black whiskers covering his cheeks. "Nonsense," she said. "His cloak's all shabby."

"But look at his shoes. Almost clean."

"So?"

"So the road to the fair's muddy. Means he was dropped off by a carriage close by. Ain't too likely for a bloke in a shabby cloak, is it?"

Clarissa considered the man curiously. "Maybe he lives close by."

"Nah. Top of his hat is wet, see? It was still raining wherever he got into his carriage." Wild Boy looked up at the clouds scudding past the moon and made a quick calculation. "Lives around London Bridge, I'd say. Lots of toffs there."

Clarissa stared at the man, then at Wild Boy. "How did you...?"

"I seen him before," Wild Boy said quickly.

"Oh. Well then you cheated. Look, he's coming this way."

They watched the man approach. With one hand, he pushed an old lady aside in his rush to get through the crowd. His other arm was stuffed inside his cloak, as if he was clutching something to his chest.

"Wonder what he's got under there?" Wild Boy said.

"Nice fat pocketbook, that's what," replied Clarissa.

They grinned at each other, and then scowled, remembering they were enemies.

"He's getting closer," Clarissa said.

The man looked like he was in a rush. Sweat dripped from beneath the brim of his top hat, and he was muttering under his breath. He stopped and looked over his shoulder, and his arm tightened around whatever he was protecting under his cloak.

"See that?" Clarissa whispered. "Definitely something under there."

She was trying to look calm, but Wild Boy could tell by the way her tongue dashed anxiously over her broken front tooth that she was as nervous as he was. Something about the man didn't seem right, although he couldn't work out what. He wanted to warn Clarissa, to tell her they should find someone else. But he reminded himself how badly he needed the money.

"Here he comes," Clarissa said.

The man came closer...

"*Now*," Wild Boy whispered.

Clarissa's hand shot under the man's cloak,

delving for a pocketbook. He was just inches away on the other side of the banner, so close that Wild Boy could see the sweat glisten on his bushy whiskers. For a thrilling second he thought Clarissa was going to pull this off…

Then the man stepped back and screamed. One hand seized Clarissa's wrist while the other lashed out, wielding a clasp knife. Unable to see his attacker, he slashed wildly at the banner. Veins bulged in his forehead as he yelled a strange warning. "You'll never get the machine! You can kill me, but you'll never get the machine!"

"Get off me!" Clarissa cried. "Get him off me!"

Wild Boy struggled to pull her from the man's grip. The knife slashed his coat sleeve, but he held on and pulled harder. Finally he tore Clarrisa free and they tumbled back between the caravans. When they looked up again, the man had turned and fled for the park gates.

All around the path, curious heads turned. Without a word Wild Boy and Clarissa sprang up and pelted away into the backstage area of the circus. They hid behind the stable hut, breathing hard.

Clarissa slammed a hand against the stable wall. "Why didn't you tell me he had a knife? He was crazy, a lunatic! And what was he saying?"

"Something about a machine," Wild Boy wheezed. "What did he have under his cloak?"

"Nothing! Just this."

She thrust a scrap of paper at his face.

It looked like a letter. Wild Boy reached out to take it, but she snatched it back.

"It's your fault," she said. "I ain't got nothing now!"

She glanced towards the circus tent and Wild Boy saw a fear in her eyes that he recognized. Clarissa, too, was scared to go back.

"Well," he said, "maybe we can find another—"

"Shut up, freak! I should never have listened to you." She shoved him in the chest and ran off towards the circus. "You owe me double now."

Wild Boy didn't bother yelling a reply. He had bigger problems than Clarissa Everett. Like her, he'd got nothing. And so he had to return to Finch. By now the showman would have passed out from drinking. But come the morning…

"I ain't scared of him," he muttered unconvincingly. "I'll punch out his teeth. Give him another scar on that ugly…"

He turned. Someone was watching him.

A dark figure stood in the shadows at the end of the stable, hidden by a sagging black hood and a leather cloak that draped to the ground. Wild Boy couldn't see anything under the cloak – no hands, no face, not even any boots through the holes in its tattered, muddy trail.

But he was certain the figure was staring at him.

He knew that drunks often sneaked behind the caravans for free looks at the freaks, but this person didn't seem like he'd been boozing. The figure stood perfectly silent and perfectly still, except where his leather shroud rustled and creaked in the wind.

Gathering his nerve, Wild Boy edged closer. "Hey!" he said. "Hey, you! Get a good look, did you?"

Still the figure didn't move. Then, from under the hood came a voice that caused Wild Boy to step back in fright. It was deep and menacing, but also strangely distant, like the growl of an animal far away.

"Where is it?" the voice said.

"Eh?"

"Where is the machine?"

"Machine?" Wild Boy replied. Wasn't that what the man he and Clarissa just robbed had yelled? *You'll never get the machine…*

A cry rang out behind him. He whirled around, but it was just someone at the fair. Quickly he turned back.

The hooded man had vanished.

"Bloomin' idiot!" Wild Boy yelled.

He tried to sound tough but something about that figure had sent a chill through every hair on his body, an even deeper fear than anything he'd experienced that night. Whoever it had been, he was glad the person was gone.

He pulled his long coat tighter around him, and trudged back towards the freak shows. He looked forward to the fair moving on, and getting out of this wretched place. So far Greenwich wasn't going well at all.

6

Wild Boy woke to the call of a crow.

The beady-eyed bird sat in the caravan doorway, considering him with a curious, tilted gaze. What was that hairy creature curled up on the floor?

The crow flapped away as Wild Boy rose with a groan from the sacks. Everything hurt from the beatings he'd taken last night – his arm, his back, his jaw. His body felt like one big bruise. He rubbed his coat sleeve and felt the slash where the man's knife had struck. It still didn't make sense to him. The man had gone crazy, screaming about some machine. And then, moments later, that hooded figure had said the same thing…

But he had to forget about it. He had a bigger problem that morning in the shape of Augustus Finch. He prayed that the showman had been too drunk last night to remember their fight.

He brushed back the hair on his face and peered nervously through the van door. Outside, the clouds had cleared and the morning sun streamed into the park. A dawn chorus of curses and threats rang out as showmen rushed around the path, setting up stalls, laying tables, readying themselves for the new day's trade. Fairground children scavenged in the mud for empty bottles to sell, while further down the path the circus porters huddled around fires, cooking bacon and heating coffee. The smells mingled in the morning breeze with the lingering odours of the previous night – spilt beer, stale sweat and pipe smoke.

Beside the van, Sir Oswald had laid breakfast on top of his clothes chest – bread with hot dripping – as well as a bowl of clean water for Wild Boy to wash. Wild Boy couldn't help smiling as he watched his friend make more improvements to their van – climbing the side with just his powerful arms, screwing a new pipe to those that already crossed the roof, and then scrambling nimbly down to connect the other end to the wheel axle. He looked focused on the work, as if it was all part of some grand plan rather than just his way of keeping busy.

Sir Oswald finally saw him, and flashed the sort of grin you didn't see often in a fairground. A friendly one. "I am glad you returned last night," he said.

Wild Boy wasn't remotely glad of the fact himself. He'd just had nowhere else to go. He tore a chunk of bread from the loaf, and nibbled the crust, scanning the fairground anxiously. "You seen Finch?" he asked.

"Fear not," Sir Oswald replied. "Mr Finch is visiting the licensor."

Relief washed through Wild Boy. On the last day of every fair, each showman had to secure a licence to trade at the next site. The next fair, Bartholomew Fair in the centre of London, was the biggest of the season, so there would be a long queue at the licensor's tent. With luck, Finch wouldn't return until moments before today's first show.

"Better do your chores," Sir Oswald said. "Don't want to upset him even further." He leaned closer and chuckled. "Took him all night to wash that toilet muck off his face."

Wild Boy couldn't bring himself to laugh. Although he was safe for now, he knew that Finch wouldn't forget about last night. Sir Oswald was right, though, there was no point in making things worse. Besides, a few chores might take his mind off things.

He did the same jobs every morning. First he cleaned the caravan floor of whatever mess the punters had made the day before – mud, booze and sometimes blood. Then he set up the stage with the crates stored under the van, propped up Finch's bed and hung the banners. Finally he fed and groomed the horses, and collected firewood for the stove.

But, that day, he couldn't shake a feeling of dread.

As he brushed the horses he glimpsed a dark shape move between the vans. And then again between the trees as he collected firewood from the corner of the park. With a shudder, he remembered the figure that had watched him last night – the mysterious hooded man.

He spotted another stick jutting from a hedge, and yanked the end. Just as it slid out, he froze.

Footsteps squelched through the grass. Someone was creeping up behind him.

Wild Boy didn't move. He didn't know if it was Finch or the hooded man, only that he had to fight. His grip tightened around the stick. He had to time this perfectly…

He whirled around, waving the stick like a sword. "Get back or I'll smash your skull!" he cried.

Clarissa Everett sprang away, just dodging the swipe. Her freckles burned bright red. "Touch me with that thing and I'll break your arms," she said.

"Break my arms and I'll break yours too!"

He wished immediately that he'd said something else. It wasn't the best line he could have used before a fight. But Clarissa's fists unclenched.

"I ain't come to fight," she said. "If I had, I'd have won by now anyhow."

The wind brushed her hair from her face, and Wild Boy spotted a dark bruise staining her pale cheek. She must have seen him look, because she turned her head. "Got it practising," she explained.

"I got a proper circus job, remember, not one in a freak show."

Wild Boy suspected she was lying. More likely the bruise was from her mother. Everyone knew that Clarissa and Mary Everett, the circus owner, didn't get on. But he reminded himself that it was none of his business, and that he hated her anyway, so he shrugged like he didn't care.

"What do you want then?" he said.

Clarissa looked around the trees, as if she too feared they were being watched. Then she brought a crumpled slip of paper from her pocket. "Look," she said.

It was the letter from last night. Wild Boy couldn't believe it – why had she kept hold of evidence of their crime? Unless… Was she setting him up for the police? He stepped back and raised his voice. "I got no idea what that is," he said.

Clarissa looked baffled. "Are you crazy? It's the letter we pinched last night. Look at it, will you."

Wild Boy stepped further away. "I never saw you last night, and I never pinched nothing in my whole life!"

Clarissa realized what he suspected. She came closer, and thrust the letter furiously at his face. "I ain't no bloody snitch! This is important. It's about murder."

Wild Boy was about to shout again, but… Did she say *murder*?

The page trembled in Clarissa's hands. "I'll read it to you," she said.

"I can read it myself," Wild Boy said, snatching it from her.

It wasn't easy. The letter was flecked with mud from last night, and the writing was badly smudged. But he finally made sense of what it said.

> I know who you are, but so does another who is after the machine. For God's sake run! Run before you are murdered!

A gust of wind rustled the trees, and the branches groaned.

"It says murder," Clarissa whispered.

"I saw what it says!" Wild Boy said.

"It was warning someone," Clarissa said. "But they never got it cos we stole it first."

"*You* stole it."

"It was both of us! What are we going to do about it?"

"Eh? We ain't gonna do nothing about it!"

"You could find out who it was written for."

"Me?"

"I asked about you. That friend of yours, the posh bloke with no legs, he said you see things that other people don't."

Wild Boy swore under his breath. "He ain't my friend!" he said. He was furious at Sir Oswald – why had he spoken to Clarissa? "And he shouldn't have been blabbing a bunch of lies," he said.

"They ain't lies. I saw it last night. You knew that man was rich just from looking at him. And you knew that family wasn't."

"I seen them before, I said."

"You're a freak *and* a liar!"

She snatched the letter back and they stood for a moment in silence. Wild Boy tried to think of a good insult, but really he didn't want to fight. He wanted to look at that letter again. The truth was he'd already seen one or two intriguing clues on it, and he was keen to know more...

But whatever this was about, he had to stay out of it. "It's none of my business," he insisted. "I got other stuff to worry about. You do an' all, with your mother."

Clarissa's freckles flared again. "You shut your head about her!" she snapped. "Ain't nothing wrong with my mother."

She threw the letter at Wild Boy. "You keep it then. But if someone *does* get killed, then it's all your fault!" She stormed away, then stopped and turned. "I know why you watch people, you know. It's because you wish you were normal like them. Well, you never will be because you're an ugly bloody freak!"

Wild Boy hurled the stick at her, but missed. He sighed – neither of them had dealt with that well, although what did he expect? They were enemies, after all. But as he picked up the letter from the ground, he couldn't resist another glance.

The machine… he read.

What was all this about?

Another gust of wind rustled the trees, and crows swooped like witches around the high branches. And then something else moved behind one of the trunks – something black and ragged, and much bigger than a crow…

Wild Boy whirled around, his heart thumping. "Who is that?" he yelled.

He rushed to the tree. But no one was there.

"Master Wild!"

Sir Oswald called from beyond the glade, one hand pressed into the grass, the other waving urgent signals. "The show's starting! Hurry!"

That was a call Wild Boy had never thought he'd be glad to hear. For the first time ever, he realized he was eager to get back inside the van. He stuffed the letter into his pocket and ran full-pelt to the fair.

7

It was the busiest day of the season so far. The road from London Bridge to Greenwich was so crowded with coaches that whip-fights broke out among the drivers. Their passengers poured through the park gates, dancing and singing in a heaving, steaming mass. The drinking tents ran out of beer, the circus sold out for each show, and queues trailed from every caravan and stall that lined the path.

Wild Boy usually hated busy days, when there was less time to spy on the fair. But today he was glad of the crowds. With so many punters, there was no chance for Augustus Finch to seek revenge for last night. But Finch hadn't forgotten. With each painful step on his wounded foot, he cast a vicious glare at Wild Boy. It was his signal that, soon enough, harm would be done.

But that afternoon, Wild Boy's mind was on

something else – the letter. Over and over he told himself to get rid of it, but he kept sneaking looks. He must have read it a dozen times that day, and it still sent a chill down his back.

Murder – it was a dark business, even for a fairground. And Clarissa was right, the warning had never been received. She was right about something else too – Wild Boy *could* tell who the letter was meant for. In fact, he thought he already knew. He kept thinking about what Clarissa had said, how it would be his fault if the person was killed. Deep down he knew she was right. If he could do something to stop it, then he had to try. But that wasn't the only reason that he'd decided to deliver the letter. It was a mystery, and he was curious to find out more.

That evening, the wind had settled and a cool mist drifted across the fairground. Wild Boy's pulse raced as he sneaked behind the caravans and around the side of the circus tent, dodging signs warning *CIRCUS CREW ONLY!* and *NO FREAKS PAST HERE!*

It was dangerous just being here. Wherever the fair travelled, freaks and their showmen always camped apart from the circus crew. It had been that way ever since the circus's star acrobat ran off with a heavily tattooed performer called the Painted Lady. That acrobat was Clarissa's father.

That was before Wild Boy's time there, but he

knew the story. Clarissa's father had been one of the best acrobats in England, and so had her mother. The three of them used to perform together, thrilling crowds in their red and gold costumes. Wild Boy had heard that those were happy times for the circus. But when Clarissa's father ran off, he left Mary Everett a bitter, broken woman. One night she walked drunk on the tightrope, fell and broke her leg. She never performed again. Instead she became the ringmaster. And she had developed a hatred of freaks that bordered on obsession.

Wild Boy dreaded to think how she'd react if she caught him sneaking around her show. But if he wanted to deliver this letter, that was where he had to go.

He peeked around the side of one of the circus's dressing vans. Close by, the big top strained in the wind against its thick tethers. From inside, he heard Mary Everett cry *Laaaadies and geeentlemen*. The last show of the day was underway.

He breathed in, steeling himself. Then he dashed for the side of the big top. He heard someone cry out, and he threw himself to the ground, sliding through the mud and under the canvas wall.

The crowd roared and, for a dreadful moment, Wild Boy feared he'd burst right into the ring. He rolled over, wiping muddy hair from his eyes. Then he saw a jumble of wooden beams above his head and knew he'd ended up in the right place – beneath the scaffold that supported the audience's seats.

"So far so good," he muttered.

He reached up and began to climb the beams. Between the audience's backs, he could just see down into the sawdust ring, where Mary Everett stood in the spluttering glare of a gas chandelier. The ringmaster leaned on a wooden crutch, bellowing at the crowd like a mad pirate. "Here's another act! Pay attention, will you!"

Before her husband ran off, Mary Everett had apparently been a beautiful woman. Wild Boy couldn't imagine it now. She had the same fiery red hair as Clarissa, except it was greasy and straggly, hanging like wet straw beneath the brim of her battered top hat. Whether she also had Clarissa's pale skin or freckles was impossible to say, for her face was covered with a thick layer of white make-up that fairground rumours said she hadn't rubbed off since the day her husband disappeared.

Wild Boy perched on a beam, waiting for one particular act. He'd never actually seen the circus show before, and couldn't believe how bad it was. Each time Mary Everett banged her crutch against a gong, another act stumbled into the ring. Drunken clowns broke into fights, trick riders messed up their tricks, and knife-throwers missed their marks with rusty blades. The audience booed. Someone even burst into tears.

The crowd settled down as, high above, Clarissa strode along a tightrope. Sequins glimmered on her costume as she jumped into a somersault and landed again on the wire with barely a wobble.

For a moment Wild Boy forgot all about the letter as he watched in amazement. Clarissa wasn't just good – she was astounding. All of the anger had vanished from her face, and her eyes sparkled with delight. Wild Boy wondered if this was her escape. Did she feel the same way doing this as he did spying on crowds?

"She ain't half bad," he muttered.

He focused his thoughts back on the letter. Most of the acts were over, which meant the person he was waiting for was due on next. He brought the letter from his coat pocket, and read it again.

> I know who you are, but so does another
> who is after the machine. For God's sake
> run! Run before you are murdered!

So who was it written for? Obviously someone who lived at the fair in disguise, but that hardly narrowed the list. There were several people here whom Wild Boy suspected lived under false identities. A more helpful question was, *who wrote it?* He'd never received a letter in his life, but he assumed they were sent between people with shared interests. And on that subject, the letter presented several clues.

1) The writer was wealthy. That was obvious from the paper, thick and grainy and clearly of fine quality.

2) The writer was a heavy drinker. A red spot on the page smelled like wine, while variations in the shade of the ink showed he'd refreshed his quill three times – unnecessary for such a short note, unless he'd paused to drink his wine.

3) The letter had been written near an open window. The ink had dried in one direction, suggesting a slight but constant breeze.

4) The writer may have conducted scientific experiments. This much Wild Boy guessed from a tiny burn mark in the corner, which was too small and precise to have been made by a flame. It could have been a coal spark, but why light a fire near an open window? He wouldn't have considered experiments as the cause, had it not been for an intriguing coincidence...

A flash of light dazzled Wild Boy. Down in the ring, a new act had begun. A man with a shabby leather bag stood beside a table that was cluttered with scientific objects – pairs of zinc and copper plates half-submerged in glasses of golden fluid, silver wires strung between copper coils, glass cylinders mounted on wooden frames. He was a crooked old man with a monk's ring of grey hair and round shaded spectacles perched on a wine-red nose.

Professor Henry Wollstonecraft.

This was the man, Wild Boy was certain, for whom the letter was meant. It had been written to someone in disguise, and he suspected that was true of the

Professor. He could tell the man had been wealthy once. His suits, now worn and crumpled, had been tailored for him and he wore an expensive-looking ring – gold with a raised letter *G* on its surface. Wild Boy wondered if that was an initial of the old scientist's *real* name...

He watched as the Professor performed tricks with a mysterious new phenomenon called *electricity*. Sparks crackled along the wires and shot into the air like white-hot fireworks, reflecting off his dark spectacle lenses. The tricks were incredible, but the Professor's act entirely lacked showmanship. When the old man finally looked up, he seemed almost surprised to see an audience, and utterly confused as to what he might say to them.

By then they'd had enough anyway, and another chorus of boos filled the big top. Still without a word, the Professor packed up his bag and shuffled away through a fading haze of smoke.

Wild Boy set off again through the scaffold. If he could climb close, he could drop the letter in the Professor's path as he left the ring. But just as he got near, his coat snagged on one of the beams. He turned to tear it free, but he was already too late. Professor Wollstonecraft passed through a gap in the tent wall and out into the night.

Wild Boy cursed. What now? Could he sneak to the Professor's caravan and leave the letter there? It was risky – if he was caught, the circus crew would think he was stealing. But this was not the sort of letter that could go undelivered. He ripped his coat from the beam, leaped from the scaffold and rushed through the exit.

It didn't take long to find the Professor's van. Because of the fire risk from his experiments, Wollstonecraft's was the only caravan at the fair that was made entirely of metal – a rusty corrugated-iron box parked among the sprawl of prop carts and dressing wagons behind the big top.

Tingling with fear and excitement, Wild Boy crept closer. He heard someone trudging along the path from the big top, and quickly hid again behind one of the carts. Peeking around the side, he was surprised to see that it was Mary Everett. Why had the ringmaster left her own show? She looked even angrier than usual. Leaning heavily on her crutch, she swore and banged a fist against one of the vans.

Every instinct told Wild Boy to run. But again he felt the page in his coat pocket. Someone was out to murder the Professor. He couldn't just let it happen.

All he needed to do was to get into that van and drop this letter. Just a few seconds, that was all – how much trouble could that cause?

As soon as the ringmaster was gone, he darted across the path, up the caravan steps and he was inside.

8

Wild Boy eased the door shut.

Moonlight streamed in silver shafts through joins in the caravan's corrugated walls. Empty wine bottles littered the floor. The air was thick with the stench of booze.

He brought the letter from his coat pocket and laid it on the floor beside the door. He knew he should leave, but again his curiosity took control. Surely there was time to snoop around a little, to see if he could find out what the letter was all about.

The van was a mess. A clothes chest lay on its side, and books were scattered among the bottles on the floor. On a work-table against the wall was a jumble of scientific instruments – test tubes filled with golden fluid, coils of silver wire wrapped around copper rods, a rat cage with metal pegs attached to its sides – and piles of papers scribbled with notes.

Edging closer, Wild Boy flicked through a few of the pages. He saw anatomical drawings of body parts – twisting muscles in an arm, a diagram of a skull, a human head bisected to expose its cauliflower brain…

The hairs bristled on Wild Boy's back. *Time to get out of here,* he decided.

He turned to leave, but stopped.

"The clothes chest," he said.

There was something strange about it – his eyes were drawn there instinctively. And now, as he stepped nearer, he realized why. The chest lay on its side, and he could see the base within. But it didn't look deep enough when compared to the panel outside.

Was it possible? His heart pounded faster as he crouched and slid a hand inside the chest. He groped the base until – *click* – one of the wooden panels hinged open.

A wide grin spread across his hairy face. There was a secret compartment.

He thought of pound notes, boxes of jewels… Whatever was in there, he'd just pinch enough to rent his own wagon, so he didn't have to go back to Finch.

His heart sank as he slid the contents out. It was just another sheet of paper, with technical diagrams and instructions for some sort of scientific contraption – a tangled sphere of cogs and pipes skewered on an axle between two wheels. Several lines, wires he supposed, trailed from the bottom of the sphere and connected to…

Wild Boy leaned closer, hoping he'd seen it wrong. But he hadn't. The wires were connected to human heads. They seemed to go *into* the heads.

THUD!

He jumped in fright, dropping the paper. Outside, something had crashed against the wall.

THUD! THUD!

Wild Boy stood very still, trying to listen over the manic thumping of his heart. He heard boots trudge through the mud. He crept to the wall and peered through one of the joins in the metal.

He couldn't see much, but there was no mistaking the crooked figure of Professor Henry Wollstonecraft, with his blood-blistered nose and shaded spectacles. The old scientist leaned against the opposite van. His golden ring glinted in the moonlight as he drank from a bottle of wine, spilling half of its contents over his crumpled suit.

Old soak, Wild Boy thought, letting himself relax. With the Professor so drunk, he could easily sneak from the van unseen. But then he heard something else.

"Henry," a voice said.

He shot to another crack in the wall. Outside, a shadow stretched long and monstrous across the mud. It was the hooded man.

Wild Boy shifted to another crack. He still couldn't

see the face under the hood. He couldn't see *anything* under that tattered leather cloak. The man moved fast, but with strange, awkward strides – loping and unbalanced, like a wounded creature. His voice was deep and vicious.

"I have come, Henry," he said.

Before the Professor could reply, the hooded man attacked. A gloved hand shot from under the cloak. It grabbed the scientist by the neck and slammed him against the van.

Finally, Wild Boy saw beneath the hood, and he had to bite his lip to stop himself from crying out. It wasn't a man that he saw, but a mask. It was one of the carnival masks that were sold around the fairgrounds – a white porcelain doll's face, eerily featureless except for a long, hooked nose, like a bird's beak, that protruded from the centre. Those masks had given Wild Boy the creeps ever since he heard they were modelled on costumes worn by plague doctors centuries ago. Masks of death, some of the showmen called them.

Behind the mask, dark eyes glinted. The tip of the porcelain beak tapped the Professor's spectacles as the hooded man leaned closer.

"Where is it?" he growled.

He struck the Professor around the face, shattering his lenses. With his other hand he lifted the old man clear off the ground. "Where is the machine?"

Blood trickled down the Professor's forehead. He

looked at his attacker through cracked black lenses. But it wasn't fear that Wild Boy saw in the man's eyes, it was sadness. Infinite sadness.

"I wish I had never built the thing," the Professor said. "It is an unholy device. No one should have that power."

"It is too late for that now, Henry," replied the hooded man.

The Professor slid a shaky hand into his pocket. "No. Not too late…"

He thrust a knife at his attacker. But he was too drunk and too weak. The hooded man twisted his hand and rammed the blade into the Professor's stomach.

Wild Boy reeled back in shock. He bashed against the workbench, and a copper rod rolled from the surface. "No!" he gasped.

The clatter of the rod echoed around the caravan. Slowly he peered again through the wall.

The hooded man was gone.

He moved to another crack, then another. Where was he? *Where the hell was he?*

The door handle turned.

Wild Boy edged back, groping for anything to use as a weapon. His hand landed on one of the jars from the work-table. He held it closer, saw golden liquid bubble inside.

The van door creaked open and moonlight trickled through. The hooded man appeared in the doorway – a ragged silhouette with a white-beaked face. "Is that you, boy?" he said. "Are you in here?"

The jar trembled in Wild Boy's hands. *Fight*, he urged himself. *Fight while you still can!*

He sprung up and hurled the liquid. It splashed over the mask, and the man stepped back in shock. Seizing his chance, Wild Boy burst past him and hurled himself through the door.

He tumbled down the caravan steps and crawled to where Professor Wollstonecraft lay curled in the mud. The old scientist's shirt was torn and sopping with blood. Sliding even closer, Wild Boy pressed desperately on the wounds. Blood soaked the hair on his hands as he pressed even harder, crying out, "Professor! Wake up! Please!"

But Professor Wollstonecraft was dead.

"Boy," a voice said.

The hooded man emerged from the caravan.

Wild Boy broke into a staggering run. He had to get help, had to tell someone what had happened. Barely thinking, he pelted past the circus pay box and into the big top. "Murder!" he cried. "There's been a murder!"

The clowns in the ring stopped tumbling and stared.

The audience in their seats stopped cheering and stared.

High above, Clarissa Everett stood on her tight-rope, and stared.

Wild Boy stumbled forward, breathless with fear. Professor Wollstonecraft's blood dripped from his hands and stained the sawdust. He couldn't stop shaking. He tried to speak, but the words didn't come out properly. "There's… Murder…"

The tent dissolved into chaos. The scaffold shuddered and screams rang out as the audience fled their seats, terrified by this creature covered in blood.

"It's a bear!" someone said.

"Is it rabid? It's rabid!"

"No!" Wild Boy said. "Listen to me…"

Someone shoved him away, and he tripped and fell into the sawdust.

"Everyone get back!" a voice roared.

Mary Everett limped into the tent, one arm leaning on her crutch. In her other arm she held a shotgun, and it was aimed at Wild Boy.

Wild Boy cowered, covering his head. "Don't shoot!" he yelled. "I ain't no animal!"

The ringmaster didn't shoot, but nor did she lower her gun. "It's no bear," she said. "It's a bloody freak."

"Please…" Wild Boy said. He was desperate to explain, but now another voice called from outside.

"Out here! Someone killed the Professor!"

"Look! This freak's got blood on him!"

"No!" Wild Boy said. "It wasn't me! Listen!"

Mary Everett squinted at Wild Boy, and the crust of white make-up cracked across her face. "I can't hear," she said. "Come closer."

"Please," Wild Boy said, scrabbling forward. "I saw what happened…"

"That's close enough," the ringmaster said.

Wild Boy knew then that he'd been tricked, and his heart broke. He tried to slide back, but he was too late.

Mary Everett swung her shotgun and smashed him in the face.

A blinding white light filled his eyes, and then everything turned red as blood trickled down his face. He saw blurry crimson visions – of the circus crew crowding around him, of Clarissa watching from her high wire, of Mary Everett peeling one of his long hairs from the barrel of her gun. Through the haze of blood, the ringmaster's powdered face looked like a raging ball of flames.

"Gather the boys," she said. "Tell them we caught the killer."

And then, everything went black.

9

Wild Boy woke in the dark.

He heard heavy, rumbling breaths. Confused, he reached out a shaky hand, feeling wooden planks beneath him and then a cold metal shaft in front. He tried to focus, but his head whirled with dizziness. He tasted blood in his mouth, panic rising in his throat. Where was he?

Yards away, something growled. He heard the soft padding of ... *paws*.

He slid forward but iron bars blocked his escape. He slid back but there were bars all around. To his horror he realized he was in a cage.

A shaft of light broke the dark. Wild Boy flinched away as the light grew into the roaring flame of a torch.

A ghastly face glared at him from the gloom – charcoal-lined eyes and crusty white make-up.

Mary Everett limped closer on her crutch, holding the crackling torch in her other hand.

"What's happening?" Wild Boy demanded. "Let me out!"

A smudge of charcoal ran like a black tear down the ringmaster's powdered cheek. "Thought you'd feel at home with the animals, freak."

She swept her torch through the dark. Its arc of flame lit a row of cages raised on wooden carts around the side of the big top. These were the homes of the circus's wild beasts – a family of cowering chimpanzees, a pair of grinning hyenas and a Bengal tiger curled against the bars, its amber eyes glinting in the torchlight.

Around Wild Boy's cage, more and more torches crackled to life. A dozen circus porters stepped from the dark. He could smell the booze on their breath, and see it in their bleary eyes.

He shuffled forward and clutched the bars. "Listen to me," he said. "There's been a murder... Professor Wollstonecraft —"

"He admits it!" said one of the porters.

"No, it weren't me!"

"Then who was it?" Mary Everett said.

"I ... I never saw his face. He wore a mask."

A ripple of laughter spread through the porters. The hyenas joined in, drool trickling from their shiny fangs.

"Enough!" said Mary Everett, and everyone shut

up – even the hyenas. "You were seen running from the Professor's van," she said. "But so was someone else. Who's your partner?"

"I ain't got no partner, I swear. It was the hooded man. Listen to me, he walks funny and he—"

The ringmaster jabbed her torch at the bars, causing a burst of sparks. Wild Boy cried out and tumbled back as the fire singed the hair on his hands and face.

Mary Everett used her torch to light a cigar. She took a long drag and blew smoke through the bars. "No, you listen to *me*, freak. You were seen running from the Professor's van. And you got blood on your hands."

Wild Boy had never been so scared. He thought of Clarissa – she knew about the letter, she could tell them why he was in the Professor's van. But he feared her mother was crazy enough to put her on trial too. Clarissa was no friend of his, but he wouldn't snitch on her.

Besides, these people didn't care what he said. They just wanted to punish a freak. He had to stay tough, look for any chance to escape. "It ain't true," he said. "You got no evidence."

A grin cracked across Mary Everett's powdered face. It was as if she'd been waiting for him to say that. "Show him," she said.

Two of the porters came forward. They took hold of the cart that held the cage and began to push it over the mud. The rest of the crew marched behind, flags of flame fluttering through the night.

Wild Boy slammed his shoulder against the side of the cage, swearing and spitting at the circus crew. "Let me out!" he yelled. "I ain't done nothing!"

But again the porters just laughed. "Haw, haw! The monkey's hungry, throw him a nut!"

They steered the cart into the long stable hut. Horses whinnied behind stall doors and whips dangled from wooden rafters. One of the porters closed the doors and stood guard. The others crowded around Wild Boy's cage – drunken, leering faces.

Too scared to fight, Wild Boy curled up in the centre of the cage and pulled his knees to his chest.

"Enough!" Mary Everett called.

The group of men parted as she came forward.

"Let the freak see," she said.

Wild Boy rose, brushing hairs from his eyes. What he saw made him gasp. "Professor Wollstonecraft!" he said.

The old scientist's body lay in a heap against the stable wall. His arms were flopped by his sides and his mouth gaped open in a silent scream. A crow pecked at his rigid fingers, and Wild Boy noticed that his golden ring was missing.

Mary Everett kicked the crow away. "You say we got no evidence," she said. "Well, how about this?"

With the end of her crutch, she flicked away some straw beside the body. Written in the mud were two words.

WILD BOY

A gust of wind sent an eerie howl through the stable.

Wild Boy tried to whisper *It wasn't me*, but the words got stuck with the fear in his throat.

Now Mary Everett used her crutch to turn one of the Professor's hands. There, on the middle finger, was a streak of mud. But there was something else too. Gripped in the corpse's stiff fingers was a clump of long brown hair.

The ringmaster looked at Wild Boy. "That yours?"

A trapdoor opened in Wild Boy's stomach, plunging panic. "No," he said. "No, I didn't do it. The hooded man set me up."

"Bloody liar!" one of the porters said.

"Shut your head!" Wild Boy yelled. "This is murder! The killer dumped the Professor's body here and set me up. Ain't it obvious?"

"How's that then?"

"Look," Wild Boy said. "See the mud on his finger? It's on his *middle* finger."

"So?"

"He wouldn't write with that finger, he'd use *this* one. And what about that hair? Look at it – it's horse hair, not mine. And what about them horses too, and all their noise tonight?"

"The horses didn't make any noise tonight," one of the porters said.

"But they would've if there was a murder done here, wouldn't they?"

Before Wild Boy knew it, his big eyes were scouring the ground for more clues. Among all the footprints, he spotted strange round impressions in the mud. They looked like marks from a walking cane, only wider and deeper.

"There!" he said. "See them marks? They go right up to the body. And look how deep they are. It was someone leaning on a cane or a stick. Remember, I told you the killer walked funny! And look! The Professor's ring is gone. He was wearing a ring when I last saw him, a gold ring with the letter G. The killer must've pinched it. But I ain't got it, do I? Search me, go on!"

A few of the porters peered at the Professor's hand curiously, but Mary Everett waved them back with her crutch.

The ringmaster puffed her cigar. "I know a few things too, freak. Know about everyone on this travelling fair. I know you stole that coat from my band, for instance. I know you hide up on the vans, spying on folk. And I'm told you can see things no one else can. Ha!"

The porters chuckled with their boss.

Mary Everett blew another cloud of smoke through the bars. "He was a clever man, the Professor," she continued. "A learned man. That's why you hated him, ain't it? Because you're just a freak and can't never be nothing else."

"No, you're wrong…"

"We heard you were seen attacking someone last night with a knife."

"What? No! He attacked *us*. *He* had the knife."

"Us? So you do have a partner. Which of the freaks is it? Tell me and maybe I'll change your sentence."

"Sentence? I ain't done nothing!"

"You ran from the Professor's van. You're covered in his blood."

"No—"

"He wrote your name."

"It ain't true—"

"You're the only monster here."

"I AIN'T NO KILLER!"

Wild Boy's cry rang around the stable. He stared at the Professor's body through watery eyes. He knew he could find more clues to prove his innocence, but what was the point? The hatred in Mary Everett's eyes was clear. And these porters wouldn't help him – they relied on her for their jobs.

But he wasn't giving up either. He reached between the cage bars to the cart's wooden floor, dug out a loose nail and gripped its end with trembling fingers. If any of these men opened the cage he would stab them with it, and try to get past. He'd spotted a hole in the stable wall that looked big enough to squeeze through.

Mary Everett turned to the porters. "One of our own has been killed," she said. "We don't need no busybody coppers around here. We take care of our own business, punish them what needs punishing. That's Showman's Law. That way everything stays right."

She looked at Wild Boy and for a moment her eyes softened. He thought he saw something like sadness under that white powder. It was almost as if she didn't want to do this, didn't want to be the person she was being. But a second later that person was back, and the ringmaster's eyes hardened.

"This is murder," she said. "Only one sentence for that. Jack, get the rope. Sam and Isaac, grab the freak."

One of the porters threw a rope around a rafter and tied the end in a noose. The others circled the cage, fire torches blazing.

Wild Boy gripped the nail, but his hands shook so hard that it slipped from his fingers. He scrambled back, feeling for the weapon. "Get away!" he warned. "Get away or you'll all be sorry!"

The porters stepped closer. And then – *whoosh* – a rush of wind extinguished their torches. The stable fell into darkness.

"Who opened the doors?" Mary Everett roared. "Joe? I said no one else comes in!"

"I am sorry," a voice replied from the dark. "It seems that Joe was remiss in his duties."

A lantern flickered to life and bobbed closer.

Wild Boy's heart surged. Had someone come to rescue him? All he could see over the porters' heads was the gleaming crown of a top hat. He dropped low and glimpsed polished black shoes and the silver tip of a cane prodding the ground. Beyond them, the porter that had guarded the stable door lay unconscious over a bale of straw.

"Who the hell are you?" Mary Everett demanded.

Finally Wild Boy saw the figure – a tall, immaculately dressed man who leaned on his cane in a way that suggested the stick was more than an accessory to his finely cut coat. As he came closer, a flash of gold shone from under the shadow of his top hat.

Slowly, calmly, the man removed the hat. The lantern light caught his face, and Wild Boy glimpsed a streak of silver and another gleam of gold. The silver was the man's hair, slicked back and perfectly parted at the side. But the gold... It was the man's eye. He had a golden eyeball.

The metal globe bulged in his thin, angular face as he looked down at the corpse of Professor Wollstonecraft. Wild Boy noticed a ring glint on the man's finger – it was just like the one the Professor had once worn, inscribed with the letter G.

The man spoke. His voice was calm and measured. "Gentlemen. You will all leave this place."

Mary Everett scoffed. "You all stay right where you are," she ordered.

Wild Boy saw her hand shake, just a little, as she

lit another cigar. Very few people made Mary Everett nervous.

"You're a copper," the ringmaster said. "You ain't wanted here. Ain't that so, fellas? Coppers don't know nothing about our world."

Wild Boy could barely believe what happened next. The golden-eyed man laughed – a great booming roar that filled the stable. Still without as much as a glance at Mary Everett, he turned and addressed one of the porters.

"You," he said, his voice now deadly serious. "Your name is Richard Carson. You are currently on parole from Newgate, where you served three years for burglary." He turned to the rest of the crew and addressed them in turn. "You are Isaac Solomon, a deserter from the French Foreign Legion. Theodore Lent, you are a part-time fence. Samuel Swales, leader of a notorious gang of grave robbers. And who could forget Mr Silas Cullen, escaped convict from the prison ship *Defiance*."

The men were speechless.

The golden-eyed man turned to the ringmaster and plucked the cigar from her mouth. "And you, Mrs Mary Louise Everett, are the holder of a circus licence that would certainly be revoked were someone to report your employees' various indiscretions."

He shoved the cigar back into her mouth. "Now, I wish to speak with the boy."

Wild Boy was as stunned as the porters. These

were rough fairgrounders, but this man spoke to them like they were children.

Several of the men rushed from the stable. The others hesitated, glancing anxiously at Mary Everett.

After a long moment, the ringmaster nodded. "You got five minutes," she said as she led the remaining porters outside.

The golden-eyed man closed the stable door behind them, and slid the bolt. The moment the door sealed, he slammed a hand against the wooden wall. He gripped his cane and grimaced, fighting some terrible agony in his head.

Wild Boy watched, astonished, as the man reached to his false eye and plucked it from his face. He gave the golden globe a shake, and then tipped some sort of liquid from inside onto his coat sleeve. He pressed the sleeve to his nose, and inhaled deeply.

His one good eye rolled upwards. The other eye's empty socket glistened in the light from his lantern as he turned and finally looked at Wild Boy. "At last," he said, "we are alone."

10

The golden-eyed man came closer, drowning Wild Boy in his shadow. Calmly he slotted his false eyeball back into its socket and shook his head to settle it in place. He smoothed back his silver hair.

"It is very important," he said, "that you remain calm."

The last thing Wild Boy felt was calm. Lashing out a leg, he kicked the cage bars. "I dunno who you are but don't you come no closer!" he warned. "I'm a monster! Ain't you heard? It was me what done the Professor, and I'll do you too if you come any closer!"

A slight smile flashed across the man's tight face. "No," he said. "You will not. Because you are lying."

"I… Eh?"

"I heard what you told the ringmaster about these marks in the mud, and the noise of the horses. It was … *unexpected*. You have quite the gift of observation. I wonder whether you could actually have convinced those men of your innocence had you not been so busy being angry."

Wild Boy's shoulders pressed against the cold cage bars. "Who the hell are you?"

"A man has been killed. I rode here as soon as I heard."

"Rode? You came by steamboat."

Again that flicker of a smile. "Interesting," the man said. "Did you observe the patch of soot on my sleeve from the ship's funnel? Or the ticket stub there in my pocket?"

Wild Boy had seen both, as well as several other clues about the man. He could tell that he had recently become a bachelor after several years of marriage, and that he had lived in India but currently resided in London, somewhere near the river. He knew he had a pistol inside his coat, a knife in his shoe, and he was fairly sure there was a sword concealed inside his walking cane. But none of that told him who this person was.

He said nothing.

"Very well," the man said. "Then I shall tell you what *I* know." He brought out a slim black notebook from his coat, and withdrew from it a crumpled sheet of paper. "You recognize this letter?" he asked.

Wild Boy shook his head, but he *did* recognize it. It was the warning letter he'd left in the Professor's van.

"This letter was composed by a colleague of mine," the man said. "He was relieved of it at this fair last night by a pair of thieves. When he informed me of this, he made a reference to a hand covered in hair, which seemed strange at the time."

"I ain't no thief. And I ain't never seen that letter."

"Look closer," the man said, and he tossed the letter into the cage.

Wild Boy snatched it up and stuffed it in his pocket. If he somehow got out of here, that letter could help prove his innocence.

He looked up, spotting something move along one of the stable rafters. At first he thought it was a cat. Then he saw a flash of red hair.

Clarissa crouched high on the narrow rafter, silhouetted against the glare of the man's lantern. She was watching.

"You are lying to me," the man said. "Let me tell you the truth. You stole that letter and you established to whom it was addressed. The burn marks, perhaps, provided the telling clue. You decided to deliver the message to Professor Wollstonecraft. It does, after all, warn of a threat upon his life. But you were too late."

He turned so that light from his lantern fell over the Professor's body. "You saw poor Henry die."

Wild Boy felt cold at the memory. He looked up, but Clarissa was gone. "I ... I dunno what you're talking about," he said.

"Then let me enlighten you."

The man turned a page of his notebook and held it open. "Look at this."

There was a drawing in the book, similar to the sketch that Wild Boy had seen in the Professor's caravan. He edged fractionally forward, scared but curious. It was a diagram of the same scientific device – wheels and pipes and interconnecting cogs, all sickeningly connected to human heads.

"What is that?" he said.

The stable door shuddered as the porters pounded against it outside. "Your five minutes is up!" Mary Everett called. "Open this door!"

The golden-eyed man tapped the drawing in his book. For the first time, a note of urgency crept into his voice. "There was a similar drawing hidden in the Professor's caravan. Now there is not. It is imperative that I find out who stole it."

Wild Boy's mind raced. The hooded man must have taken the drawing. That was why he'd dumped the body here in the stables, so he could search the Professor's van without being seen.

The porters banged harder on the stable door. Wild Boy had to take a chance.

"All right, listen," he said. "I did see the drawing. It was in the Professor's van. I was only there to leave that letter, not to steal nothing. That was when I saw the killer, the hooded man."

The man's jaw tightened. A silver hair fell in front

of his false eye and he slicked it back. "The hooded man?"

"That's who killed the Professor. He must've taken that drawing an' all."

"Who was he?"

"You think I'd be here if I knew that? I didn't see his face, nor nothing else of the bloke. He walked funny, like he was hurt. And he wore a mask, like them ones what—"

"Did he speak?"

"I… Yeah, yeah, he spoke."

"What did he say?"

"I dunno… Something about some machine."

The hair slipped again over the man's eyes but this time he let it hang. He looked back to Professor Wollstonecraft's corpse. "Then it is true," he said.

"What's true?" Wild Boy said. "Only thing that's true is I'm about to get hung. I told you what I know, so get me out of here."

The man tucked his notebook away and brought out a slim leather pouch that was folded shut like an envelope. "It is imperative," he said, "that I identify this hooded man."

"I told you everything I know."

"No. You told me everything you *think* you know."

The man opened the pouch. Something glinted inside. A syringe.

"What's that?" Wild Boy said. "What the hell's that for?"

"You are afraid," the man said. "You are not thinking clearly. I suspect you saw more than you remember."

The syringe's bronze tip reflected in his golden eye, and pale liquid dripped from the needle point. "This drug will *make* you remember."

If Wild Boy hadn't been so scared he might have laughed. There was no way he was letting anyone stick him with a needle. He scrambled back, kicking again at the bars. "Get back! Don't you touch me with that thing!"

"It will be less painful if it enters your arm," the man said. "But it does not have to."

Another thump shook the stable doors. "Give us the boy!" one of the porters yelled. "Showman's Law for him!"

Wild Boy turned in the cage, searching desperately for the floorboard nail he'd dropped. He saw it on the straw outside the cage, but it was too far to reach. Only one other plan came to mind.

Shifting around, he slid his coat down to offer the man a hairy, trembling shoulder. "All right," he said. "Use your needle. But stick it in my arm like you said."

The golden-eyed man hesitated, suspicious. But he wasn't missing his chance. Holding the syringe steady, he leaned closer. "I am afraid," he said, "that this will hurt."

Wild Boy braced, waiting. He had to time this just right...

Now!

He slammed his palm into the loose end of the floorboard. The other end shot up through the bars and caught the man hard on the chin. The man's golden eyeball fell from his face as he toppled back and collapsed to the floor.

Again the porters banged the doors. The rafters shook. The horses stamped and reared in their stalls.

Wild Boy lay flat in the cage and reached for the nail. If he could grab it, maybe he could pick the lock to the cage. His fingers were tantalizingly close, but it was just beyond his grasp. "Come on," he begged. "Please…"

And then – *thump!* – two feet landed on the straw beside the nail.

Clarissa!

Beneath a long, dark coat, the red and gold sequins of her circus costume shimmered in the lamplight. She looked at Wild Boy, and her tongue flicked nervously across her broken tooth. "I heard what you said about the hooded man," she said. "You didn't snitch on me to my mother. You could've, but you didn't."

Wild Boy gripped the bars, his heart surging with fresh hope. "Yeah, so now you're gonna get me out of here."

Clarissa looked at the stable door, heard her mother order the porters to smash it down. She touched the bruise on her face, scared, unsure.

"Clarissa, I swear I won't tell your mother. She won't beat you or —"

"Shut your head about my mother! She ain't never beaten me!"

Wild Boy knew she was lying. He had to convince her that this was bigger than the fight between her and her mother. He knew that, as well as being an acrobat, Clarissa's father had performed escape-artist tricks in the circus show. Perhaps he'd taught her some of his skills.

"Clarissa, see that rope? Your mother is gonna hang me from it. She's gonna *hang me*, Clarissa. Please use that nail. Try to open the lock."

"It won't work," Clarissa said.

"What?"

"That lock's a Smithson. Can't pick a Smithson with a nail."

Wild Boy swore, kicked the bars. "Try, will you? Please!"

"Won't work with a nail," Clarissa insisted. She slid a leather pouch from her coat pocket. "I got my father's old lock picks though."

Wild Boy stared for a second – had she always intended to rescue him? He banged a hand on the bars, delighted. "That's great! Now use them!"

Her hands shook as she selected two of the thin iron slips from the pouch and slid them into the lock. Metal rattled against metal.

"Hurry," Wild Boy urged.

"I am hurrying!"

"I know, but hurry faster!"

Then – *clunk!* – the lock turned. Wild Boy cried out in joy as the cage door swung free. He leaped through and landed beside Clarissa in the straw.

And then the stable door burst open. The porters staggered inside, stopping when they saw the scene – the golden-eyed man unconscious on the ground, Wild Boy free from the cage and Clarissa beside him with the lock picks in her hand.

Mary Everett stood among them, staring, aghast. Again Wild Boy thought he saw the ringmaster's hard eyes soften, as if she was fighting against a kinder person inside. Then she looked at her daughter with *the freak*.

Clarissa reached out a shaking hand. Tears glistened in her eyes. "Mother," she said. "I —"

"Get them," the ringmaster growled. "Get *both* of them."

Wild Boy couldn't leave Clarissa, not after what she'd just done. He grabbed her arm to pull her with him, but she resisted. Still she stared at her mother, as the ringmaster approached with the mob.

"Come on!" Wild Boy said. "I know a way out."

But now something grasped the tail of his coat. It was the golden-eyed man. His silver hair hung around his face, and blood oozed from a cut above his empty eye socket. "Do not run!" he said. "You are in danger! Great danger!"

Wild Boy tore free and ran for the wall. Clarissa followed, fleeing for her life from her own mother.

"Go!" Wild Boy said, pushing her through the hole in the wood. As he climbed after her, he heard the golden-eyed man crying out, and he knew the man was right. They were indeed in great danger.

And now they had to run.

11

Wild Boy ran.

In among the sprawl of vans behind the circus, slipping over, staggering up. Wind whipped at his eyes and dried his tears. Caravan doors burst open. Voices rang out, horrified, confused.

"What is it?"

"One of the freaks killed the Professor. That one with the hair."

"There! It's there! Grab it!"

"There's two of them! It's Clarissa an' all!"

Clarissa raced up beside Wild Boy as he hid behind one of the vans. She was breathing hard and shaking, her face as pale as snow. "What do we do now?"

Close by, a gang of showmen charged past, heading for the big top.

"Quick," Wild Boy whispered.

As soon as the men had gone, he darted around the side of the van and scrambled breathlessly up the ladder. Clarissa came up after him and they lay flat against the rain-slicked roof, sides pressed together. Wild Boy could feel her heart beating even harder than his as they listened to the circus crew run past on the path below.

And then they heard something else.

Dogs – coming closer.

"Your crazy mother's set the hunting dogs on us!" Wild Boy gasped.

The porters must have given the dogs a smell of the Professor's blood, and Wild Boy was covered in the stuff. He bolted upright, rubbing frantically at the blood on his hands, tearing thick clumps of bloody hair from his skin. But there was too much blood, too much hair.

They needed to get away from those dogs, but there was no way they could escape on the ground. There *had* to be another way out.

Clarissa was no help. Her gaze was fixed on the big top. She didn't look like she could move, let alone escape. Wild Boy thought about leaving her, but she had helped him escape when she didn't have to, and because of that she was on the run too.

"The roofs," he said. "We can use the caravan roofs."

He turned and looked across the roofs of dozens of vans parked behind the big top. There were only a few feet between each – they could use them as stepping-stones to reach the edge of the park. Beyond was a street and a muddle of houses. Maybe they could find somewhere there to hide.

Behind, the barking grew louder. The dogs raced closer.

"You coming?" Wild Boy said.

"I… I'm coming…"

"Then let's go."

He ran across the roof and jumped.

THUMP!

He landed heavily on the next caravan, windmilling his arms to stop himself skittering off the edge. He recovered his balance and jumped again, then again and again, springing over the dark crevasses between the vans. Each time he landed he heard plates smash inside, people crying out in alarm.

THUMP! THUMP! THUMP!

Clarissa overtook him in moments, leaping the gaps with ease. "Hurry!" she cried.

Ahead, Wild Boy saw carriages on the street at the edge of the park. They were getting closer, but so were the porters. He glimpsed the men as he flew over their heads. Hands snatched at him. Fingers swiped.

"They're up on the roofs!" someone shouted.

"Get the dogs over here!"

Clarissa landed on the next caravan, and stopped. "No—" she breathed.

One of the porters stood on the next roof, blocking the way. The man had a meat cleaver in his hand and a bad smile on his pockmarked face. "I got them!" he called.

Dogs reared at the side of the van, snarling and slavering.

"Get back!" Wild Boy yelled at the man. "Get back or I'll tell your wife about your mistress."

The porter, and Clarissa, stared at him. Only now did Wild Boy understand what he had said. Before he'd even realized, his eyes had sought out clues to use against the man.

"Your wedding ring," he said. "See the line where you've taken it off tonight? And that stain on your collar is lipstick. I seen your wife, Jack, and she don't wear lipstick. Let us go and we won't say nothing. Ain't that right, Clarissa?"

"I… Yeah, that's right."

The porter looked at them, dumbfounded. Then, very quietly, he stepped aside.

Wild Boy and Clarissa leaped to the next roof and kept going. They could see the edge of the park now, enclosed by a hedge about thirty yards from the last van, and the carriages rattling by on the other side. Lights teased from the houses beyond. They were getting closer.

Clarissa jumped from the top of the last van, somersaulted in the air, landed below. "Hurry!" she screamed.

But then Wild Boy saw something awful.

A porter charged into the caravan below. He was carrying a shotgun.

BOOM!

Wild Boy barely knew what happened next. One moment he was on top of the van, and the next he was sprawled in a pile of straw on the ground. Slowly, his senses came back into focus, and a sharp pain screamed in his shoulder. His coat was torn, and blood flowed from a gash in his arm.

Clarissa leaned over him, trying to pull him up. "Get up! Get up or I'll leave you!"

He heard the dogs barking, the circus crew shouting. He had to keep going. Clutching his wound, he staggered after Clarissa towards the hedge.

He dived through the first gap he saw and tumbled onto the street. A carriage thundered towards him, passing so close that its wheels brushed the hair on his face. Carriages flew by, packed with people leaving the fair. One of the horses saw Wild Boy and reared in panic. Its coach skidded across the road and slammed into a lamppost. The driver yelled curses but Wild Boy and Clarissa were already gone.

They raced down an alley between the houses, and into a dingy scullery yard. Snarls echoed around the walls, as if the dogs were coming from all directions.

Wild Boy turned and looked around the houses. He saw high walls, drainpipes, and gutters kissing gutters above. This place was a climbing frame for someone like Clarissa, but not him, not injured. The idea of going on alone made his stomach churn with fear, but he knew what they had to do. Without him she could escape.

"We gotta split up," he said.

"What? No, we don't need to run. You can get us out of this, can't you? You can find clues, prove that we're innocent."

They locked tearful, desperate eyes. Wild Boy wondered if it was possible. He *wished* it was. But he shook the thought away. No one would listen to what he had to say – he was just a freak.

"They're coming now," he said. "You gotta run."

She didn't move – she was too scared.

Wild Boy didn't look at her again, in case he lost the courage to go on alone. Instead, he turned and ran in the other direction down another alley, shaking all over from pain and panic. He tried to scramble up a wall, but a bolt of agony shot from his wounded arm. He tumbled down and splashed into a stream of filth that trickled down the alley.

"Sewage..." he muttered.

In an instant he knew what to do. He ran on through the alley, his eyes raking the cobbles until he spotted a brown stream gushing into an open drain. The drain fed into the sewers, and the dogs wouldn't smell him if he was covered in sewage.

Tendrils of rotten-smelling gas rose from the

depths. But now was no time to be squeamish. Now was the time to survive. He held his breath, and dived into the hole.

Brown muck sprayed at his face as he slid through the slurry. His cry was cut short by a sudden drop and a splash-landing in sludgy water. He came up spitting, swearing, wiping the hairs on his face. He couldn't hear the dogs any more.

Too tired to go on, he leaned his injured shoulder against the sewer wall. His coat was torn and his wound was smeared with filth. He looked away from the infected mess, struggling to stop himself from crying.

Don't you cry. Don't you bloody cry…

But he couldn't hold back the tears. He clamped a hand over his mouth as they escaped in gulping, gasping sobs.

His head swam. Terrifying visions loomed from the dark – the hooded man's sinister beaked mask, Professor Wollstonecraft curled up in the mud, and the golden-eyed man warning him, *"You are in danger! Great danger!"*

Wild Boy forced another step but his legs buckled and he sank to his knees in the sewage. He reached for the wall, making another effort to walk. But it was too much.

He slumped forward into the waters, his long coat splayed across the curdled surface.

PART II

The WILD BOY OF LONDON

& THE FAIRGROUND FIEND

Clarissa Everett

12

South London, Night

A trickle of slime stole down a wall, glistening in a slant of moonlight that fell between the nodding shed-like houses. It slipped between the cobbles, gathering as it went the particles of waste spattered across the street – gobbets of phlegm, flecks of vomit, the reeking overspill from domestic cesspits.

The filth of the street percolated down. It nudged at the ceiling of an ancient sewer, crept through a crack in the crumbling mortar. It hung from the bricks in a single fat drop. Then it fell and landed – *pat!* – on the head of a small boy covered in hair.

Wild Boy opened his eyes.

Everything was black. Not a crack of light any-where. He was lying on his back on what felt like wet cloth. He heard dripping water, although his mouth was dry and tasted like mould. He extended a foot cautiously into the darkness, felt cold slime on broken brick. He tried to stay calm, but panic over-whelmed him.

"I didn't do it," he gasped. "It wasn't me…"

He scrunched his eyes shut and prayed that when he opened them he'd be back at the fair and everything would be normal.

He opened his eyes and gazed heartbroken around the sewer. He was lying on a narrow ledge that ran along the tunnel wall. Someone had taken his coat, and the hairs on his body were stiff with dried sewage. His injured shoulder, though, had been cleaned and wrapped in bandages. Had he been captured or rescued?

Slish, slosh…

Something moved in the sewage.

Wild Boy sat up and stared into the arched darkness. He heard liquid dripping from above. He heard his own shallow breaths getting deeper and faster with fear. And then, there it was again – a slow sloshing sound echoing off the curving walls. Was it a rat?

"… Wild Boy… "

That was no rat. Someone was coming this way. He had to get up and move.

He slid from the ledge and dropped into a river of stinking slush. Foul water soaked his hair as he groped through the dark, crawling away from the voice.

"Hear that?" the voice said.

"Hear what?" another replied.

"Swear I heard something up ahead. Gimme the knife."

The voices grew louder, closer. Wild Boy was too dazed to escape. He had to fight. Whoever these men were, they sounded almost as scared as him – maybe he could catch them by surprise. If he screamed and ran at them they might turn and flee. He braced himself, shaking with fear, as they came even closer.

Now, he thought. *Now!*

He opened his mouth to scream – but then a hand shot from the dark and smothered his cry.

"Keep silent," someone whispered in his ear.

Wild Boy tried to pull away, but the hand tightened around his mouth, almost crushing his jaw. A wrinkled face leaned closer. "They're after you, Master Wild. Bounty hunters."

It was Sir Oswald! Wild Boy cried out again, but this time in delight. He had never been so relieved to see another person. He wanted to ask what was happening, but now his friend gripped his arm and guided him into an alcove in the wall. Sir Oswald slid in after him and huddled close, resting the stumps of his thighs on Wild Boy's lap.

In the tunnel, the footsteps came closer.

Wild Boy's eyes had become used to the darkness and could just make out the squat shapes of two men crouched low as they waded past.

The man at the back sounded nervous. "What if Wild Boy *is* down here?"

"Then we're rich!" his partner replied. "Ain't that the point? Reward's doubled this past week."

Reward? Week? But Wild Boy stayed silent. He waited, deadly still, until the men had passed and their voices were a distant echo in the dark.

Sir Oswald shifted from Wild Boy's lap and gave his knee a cheery pat. "That was a wheeze, eh? Come on, they might turn back."

Wild Boy didn't follow. He pulled his knees to his chest and curled up tight, wishing the darkness would swallow him. "Sir Oswald?" he said. "What are you doing here? What's happening? That man said they'd been after me for a *week*."

"Been in a fever, old chap. That wound of yours got infected. Wasn't sure you'd make it at first. Should have known a tough chap like you would pull through, eh?"

"But I ain't no killer. I gotta tell the coppers."

"Out of the question, I'm afraid."

"Sir Oswald, I gotta tell someone what really happened."

Sir Oswald turned on his palms. When he spoke again, it was in a voice that Wild Boy had not heard from him before – deep and serious and full of force. "Master Wild, you are the target of the largest man-hunt this city has seen since Jack Sheppard. If you go back up there, the mob will kill you in the street. And the police... I'm afraid they will hang you as soon as look at you."

He clapped his hat on his head and grinned. "Good news is, it's almost time for supper."

Wild Boy sat in the alcove as Sir Oswald splashed away. He wished desperately that he could convince people of his innocence. He wanted to climb back to the street and scream it until they believed him. But Sir Oswald was right – it was too dangerous. He needed a plan, a way out of this, although his mind spun with fear and confusion, and he couldn't think straight.

At least he wasn't alone. There was a reward on his head, and most people he knew would sell their own mothers for a few pence. But he could trust Sir Oswald, he was sure. With a heavy heart, he set off after him into the dark.

13

Something rotten squelched under Wild Boy's hands as he crawled through a hole in the sewer wall. A puff of foul-smelling gas rose at his face, making his head whirl and his stomach turn. He gagged and spat in disgust.

"Where are we going?" he spluttered.

"Somewhere safer," Sir Oswald replied. "I would have moved you sooner, but I feared for your fever. Damned bad one it was too. You kept babbling about some machine. No, *the* machine, I think it was. Whatever was the meaning of that?"

Wild Boy grunted, pretending not to know. But he did, all too well. *The machine* – that was why the hooded man had murdered Professor Wollstonecraft. He was after some sort of machine. The golden-eyed man had spoken of it too. Wild Boy wished he knew more, something he could tell the police to prove his innocence.

"Watch your head," Sir Oswald said.

The tunnel ended in an abandoned basement. A fire smouldered in the corner, and shadows squirmed on bare brick walls. Thin stalactites of filth hung from the low ceiling, dripping brown liquid to the black floor.

At the side of the chamber was a dinner table made from objects salvaged from the sewers – a corrugated-iron sheet with newspaper napkins and broken bases of oil lamps as bowls. A candle flick-ered between them, dribbling wax onto the sack tablecloth.

Sir Oswald stirred a pot of food over the fire. "It is not exactly St James's Palace," he said, "but we shall make do."

Wild Boy couldn't help smiling. Good old Sir Oswald, always making the best of a bad situation. He spotted his coat by the fire. The sleeves were stiff with dried sewage, and there was a tear over the shoulder, but as he slid it on he immediately felt better.

"Where are we?" he asked.

"Somewhere under Bermondsey, I think. Wretched district. You two are much better off down here."

Wild Boy turned. "Two?"

Clarissa Everett stepped from the gloom. Under-ground, the acrobat's face seemed paler than ever. She looked anxiously at Wild Boy, and the bandage on his shoulder. "Are you...?" She turned to Sir Oswald. "Is he all right?"

Sir Oswald nodded. "He is indeed, largely thanks to your—"

Suddenly Clarissa stormed up to Wild Boy and jabbed him hard in the chest. "This is your fault!" she yelled. She was so close that flecks of her spit wet the hair on his face. "I should be in the circus tonight, but instead I'm wanted for murder."

Wild Boy stepped back, clutching his bandaged shoulder. "Circus?" he said. "It's them that's after you! If your bloomin' mother hadn't—"

"Shut your head about her! She didn't understand."

"Some misunderstanding! She set dogs on us!"

"And I wish they'd caught you!"

Wild Boy was about to shove her, but Sir Oswald rushed between them. "Master Wild! Miss Everett! Listen here, I have been in tighter squeezes than this and ridden out with the colours. Ridden with the Iron Duke, by gad!"

"Tell her, if she touches me again," Wild Boy said, "she'll be eating sewage."

"Master Wild, that is no way to address a lady. Besides, you owe Miss Everett a debt of gratitude. Not only did she save you from the circus crew, but she is also responsible for your rescue down here."

Beneath his hair, Wild Boy's face reddened. He'd

assumed that Sir Oswald had found him and saved his life. "What?" he said.

Clarissa shrugged. "I bumped into Sir Oswald after we split up. It was his idea to find you though. I'd have left you here to drown."

"Poppycock!" Sir Oswald said. "And, Miss Everett, may I remind you that, as you told me, Master Wild insisted that you run off to save yourself. An entirely noble gesture."

"I was just sick of her moaning," Wild Boy said.

"Enough, both of you. We can discuss what to do over dinner."

Sir Oswald carried the cooking pot to the table, waddling awkwardly on the stumps of his thighs. He spooned thick green gunk into the bowls. It was pea soup, and it smelled wonderful. Wild Boy plonked himself at the table.

"Master Wild! It is customary for a gentleman to allow a lady to sit first."

"Don't see no lady, just her."

Clarissa scowled. "And I don't see no gentleman, just a freak."

Sir Oswald tucked his newspaper napkin into his collar. "Well, *bon appétit*."

For several minutes the only sound in the chamber was slurping as they drank their soup. Between sips, Wild Boy snatched glances at Clarissa. He saw her hand tremble when she raised her spoon, the redness of her eyes and the salty tracks that stained her cheeks. He couldn't blame her for crying – he could still picture her mother growling, *"Get them. Get both of them."*

Clarissa slammed her spoon on the table. "I wish I'd never let you free!" she yelled.

"Why did you then?" Wild Boy said. "I didn't need your help!"

"I wish I'd never!"

"You never shoulda! You look out for yourself and that's all."

"Master Wild!" Sir Oswald said. "This is no time for high spirits. Need I remind you that whoever killed those men remains at large? Do you have any idea who the person was?"

Wild Boy felt a sudden sickness in his stomach, and not because of the soup. "What men?" he said.

"Excuse me?"

"You just said whoever killed *those men*."

Sir Oswald patted his lips with his newspaper bib. "Ah, well…"

"Show him," Clarissa said.

"Show me what?"

"Well," Sir Oswald mumbled. "I had hoped to wait until you regained your strength…"

"Just show him!"

With a defeated sigh, Sir Oswald pulled the newspaper bib from his collar. He passed the grease-stained sheet across the table. "Yesterday's *Chronicle*," he said. "But I wouldn't let it upset you,

Master Wild. It's… Well, it is probably a pack of lies."

Wild Boy took the crumpled page. At first he was too scared to look. But he had to know what was going on. Pulling the candle closer, he began to read.

14

SECOND WILD BOY MURDER – DETAILS EMERGE

New particulars have come to light with regard to the gross and violent murder of Doctor Charles Ignatius Griffin, which has gripped the entire city since its perpetration three days ago.

The murder of Doctor Griffin, combined with that of circus performer Professor Henry Wollstonecraft, has thrown the city into a state of panic the like of which has never been witnessed. The particulars of the crime are as follows: on the evening of Wednesday 27th October, Doctor Griffin was alone at the house which was both his home and his medical college on Tooley Street, in the borough of Southwark, when sometime around eleven o'clock, several students who lodged at nearby premises claim to have heard a scream from inside the building.

The gentlemen rushed to the house, but found no evidence of a break-in.

All the doors were locked and bolted from the inside, and there was no sign that any of the windows had been forced.

At that moment another scream was heard and the gentlemen immediately forced the door upon its hinges. No further sounds were heard, but when the gentlemen ventured to the third floor of the house, the full wickedness of the crime was revealed.

Doctor Griffin was discovered laid upon a table in the classroom, having been murdered in a most shocking manner. Upon closer examination, the identity of his assassins was discovered written upon a wall in the doctor's blood. All of the gentlemen present are in agreement that the words written were as follows:

WILD BOY AND CLARISSA
DONE IT.

The alarm was raised, but the gentlemen were unable to locate the miscreants anywhere on the premises, and neither were the police able to establish the means by which the killers had gained entry into the house, which was locked from within. There is little doubt, however, that the assassins were the creature Wild Boy and his partner, Clarissa Everett, who continue to elude capture and pervert justice in a most hideous manner.

The concern of Londoners could not be greater had the Devil himself committed these crimes. Police released the following description of Wild Boy: around 4 feet 5 inches tall, slim build, covered entirely in thick brown hair, red military jacket, bad trousers, no boots. Also known as the Wild Boy of London and the Beast of Bermondsey. Clarissa Everett is described thus: red hair, red freckles, sequinned red and gold circus attire. Also known as the Fairground Fiend.

The police have stressed that no pains will be spared to bring these killers to swift and public justice.

The paper trembled in Wild Boy's hands. He read it again, barely able to believe what it said. It was just like at the fair – he'd been set up, his name written at another murder scene. But he didn't even *know* this new victim.

Anger boiled through him. Just because he was a freak, everyone believed that he was guilty. Unable to control himself, he grabbed one of the soup bowls and hurled it against the wall of the underground chamber. He leaned over the table, swearing and pulling the hair on his face.

"Finished feeling sorry for yourself?" Clarissa said.

"No, I ain't," Wild Boy spat. "Leave me alone, will you?"

"I will not! My name's at that house an' all, you know? And you're going to help me get out of this."

"Yeah? How am I gonna do that?"

"We're going to find clues to prove we're innocent."

Sir Oswald collected the remaining bowls. "Listen to her, Master Wild. She speaks sense."

"It was his idea really," Clarissa said, nodding at Sir Oswald. She prodded Wild Boy's arm. "That's your skill, ain't it? Seeing things."

"I ain't got a skill."

"Master Wild," Sir Oswald said. "It is poor form to lie to a lady. Perhaps, were you not so busy being angry, you might use your abilities to solve this mystery. Indeed, were you and Miss Everett to put aside your differences, I believe that you would make a formidable duo. Why, you even look like partners already."

He gestured to their clothes – Wild Boy's long crimson tunic with its gold tassels, and the red and gold sequined dress under Clarissa's coat. "A detective and an acrobat," he said. "Yes, a quite formidable duo."

"I can pick locks an' all," Clarissa added.

"Good for you," Wild Boy muttered.

He knew it was a silly thing to say. The truth was, he felt embarrassed. He'd always prided himself on being a survivor, but so far all he'd done was shouted at Clarissa. At least she wanted to do something about this. But he knew her plan wouldn't work. "Ain't no point trying to prove our innocence," he said.

"Why ever not?" Sir Oswald said.

"Because no one will listen. See this?" He threw the news sheet across the table. "The Wild Boy of London. A monster with a price on my head. All anyone will care about is the reward. They don't wanna hear about our innocence."

"Great!" Clarissa said. "So you just wanna sit here and get caught. We ain't friends, but I thought you were tough at least."

"I ain't saying we do nothing."

"Then what are you saying, Master Wild?" Sir Oswald asked.

Wild Boy thought for another moment, wondering if his plan was right. They couldn't hide down here forever, even with Sir Oswald's help. The bounty hunters would flush the tunnels, drown them in the darkness. At best they'd get caught and only have their word to give the police.

"We go after the killer," he said. "We find out who he is, and we catch him."

Sir Oswald looked alarmed. "Master Wild, surely it would be more sensible to investigate those clues that you know. Miss Everett said the killer was after a machine of Professor Wollstonecraft's. And she spoke of an individual with a golden eye. Perhaps you could pursue one of those leads, or —"

"No," Clarissa interrupted. "I like his plan. We owe the killer anyhow. Revenge, right?"

She looked at Wild Boy, and it was as if her eyes lit that fire again inside him. They may not have been friends, but they were both fairgrounders and they had a score to settle.

"Revenge," he agreed.

"Then we need to make a list," Clarissa decided. "Things we know about the killer. Got any paper?"

Wild Boy dug in his pocket, brought out the warning letter from Greenwich Fair. He and Clarissa looked at it for a moment, wishing they'd never seen the thing. But it was too late now. "Write on the back," he said.

Clarissa dipped one of her lock picks in the muck on the wall, and used it as a quill to compose her list. "First," she said, "you thought the hooded man walked funny."

"Yeah, but he's fast and strong an' all."

"Master Wild," Sir Oswald said. "Did you recognize the killer's voice?"

"No. It was muffled by his mask. But he knew the Professor, called him Henry. Stole his ring too."

Clarissa scribbled that on her list. "And there were cane marks around the Professor's body, right?"

"I dunno," Wild Boy replied. "They *looked* like cane marks…"

"Anything else, Master Wild?"

Wild Boy cast his mind back to the fair. The images were frozen perfectly in his memory. He closed his eyes and studied them for clues.

"The killer's cloak," he said. "There were creases in the leather. That means he screws it up to store. But he doesn't fold it, so he must take it off in a rush and hide it. And the hood had marks from where it had brushed a low ceiling. There were lots of them, so he brushes that ceiling often. Could be where he lives – a low-roofed place, small and cheap."

Clarissa looked at Wild Boy, astonished by his recall. Then she shrugged, made another note on her list, and shoved it in her pocket. "Well then, you do the clues and I'll think about how we catch him."

Sir Oswald clapped his hands. "I suggest you begin at the house of this second victim, Doctor Charles Ignatius Griffin. Perhaps you will find a clue there to track down the killer."

Clarissa sprung up. "Let's go!"

"I fear it won't be that easy, Miss Everett," Sir Oswald warned. "The Doctor was killed at his college in Southwark. That is over a mile away, and half of the city is after you."

A chill ran through Wild Boy that had nothing to do with the cold. Southwark – he knew that place. That was where his old workhouse was, a grim brick building that overlooked the Thames. He'd sworn he'd never go back there. Only now he had no choice.

"The sewers," he said. "We can go underground until we get near the river. Then we'll be close."

"It's a damned risky go," Sir Oswald said, "but I smell adventure. I shall travel overground and scout for danger. We shall begin at first light."

Wild Boy had no idea when first light was. Down here everything was black or brown. He pulled his coat around him and curled up beside the fire as the dying embers pulsed orange and red in the draught.

But he couldn't sleep. Spying on people at the fair was one thing, but this was something bigger, and much more dangerous. Scared as he was though, he was excited too. The details in the newspaper report about the locked house intrigued him. It was that same feeling that had led him to Professor Wollstonecraft's caravan at the fair. A puzzle waiting to be solved. Only, could he really solve it?

He had to. Because if he couldn't, he and Clarissa were as good as dead.

15

Wild Boy crouched beside the drain cover, ready to dive back into the sewer at the slightest hint of danger in the street. Somewhere close, a dog barked. Glass broke. A woman screamed. And then silence, except for the sound of his filthy coat dripping onto the greasy cobbles.

He reached to help Clarissa up from underground, but she swatted his hand away as she climbed from the drain. They'd been on the move for hours, hacking and retching through the stinking darkness. Only when they'd climbed a drain shaft and seen a sign for Tooley Street did they know they'd reached Southwark, where the hooded man's second victim had lived – Doctor Charles Ignatius Griffin.

A thick brown cloud swept along the street. Wild Boy remembered fogs like this from when he'd lived at the workhouse. These sickly brews of coal smoke and factory fumes shrouded the riverbank nearly every night, bringing confusion and fear. But as the clouds swirled around them, Wild Boy and Clarissa grinned. Thanks to the fog the streets were empty – for now.

As they looked at each other, their smiles turned into laughs that echoed around the thick fumes. Partly they were relieved to have made it this far. But also they both looked so *revolting*. Brown slime dripped from Clarissa's hair. It was all over Wild Boy too – sliding down his coat, and soaking the hair on his face and body. They looked like monsters risen from a swamp.

"Over there," Clarissa said.

They rushed to a horse trough and dunked their heads in the water, then tore off their coats, splashed their arms and rubbed their faces. Soaked through, Wild Boy shook himself like a dog, spraying mucky water over Clarissa.

"Hey!" she cried.

She grabbed the trough-bucket, about to hurl more water over him, but she froze mid-swing. A curtain of fog parted long enough to see the wall behind the trough. It was covered with posters, each with the same printed announcement:

£100 REWARD
FOR THE CAPTURE OF
The ★★★ WILD BOY ★★★ OF LONDON
★ & The FIEND ★
Clarissa Everett

Clarissa dropped the bucket. "Fiend," she said. "Is that like a ghost?"

Wild Boy heard voices. Quickly he pulled Clarissa into an alley between two buildings.

Slowly they dared a look. Through the fog, they saw several men silhouetted against the jaundiced light of a street lamp, dressed identically in high-collared coats and stovepipe hats. At the base of the lamp was something ragged and black, like a crow.

"Sir Oswald's cravat," Clarissa said.

They'd agreed that Sir Oswald would go ahead and tie his cravat around the lamppost nearest to where Doctor Griffin had lived and worked. The house he'd signalled rose higher than those around it – four floors of brick and glass covered in so much soot and grime from nearby factory chimneys that its entire face seemed to drip with darkness. Wrought-iron railings ran along the front, like prison bars guarding the ground floor windows.

"Who are them people outside it?" Clarissa said.

"Coppers," Wild Boy said, and cursed. They had to get inside that house.

But before he could think what to do, Clarissa turned and ran off – a blur of red and gold charging down the alley. "I got a plan. Follow me."

Wild Boy chased after her, whispering for her to slow down, but she was in her element now. She swept along the back of the houses, back-flipped over a fence and vaulted a wall.

"Hurry up!" she called.

He caught up with her in a small yard surrounded by high walls. Brightly coloured handkerchiefs hung on a washing line, fluttering in the fog, and the voices of the policemen echoed down an alley that trailed along the side of the building. A shiver of excitement ran up Wild Boy's spine. This was Doctor Griffin's house.

Clarissa was already at the back door, fiddling her picks in the lock. "It's bolted from the inside," she said. "This window's barred an' all."

Wild Boy moved closer, intrigued by the iron bars that protected the window. He ran a finger around the mortar where the metal met the window ledge. "These bars are new," he said.

"So?"

"So the Doctor was scared of something."

"But how did his killer get in?"

Wild Boy stepped back and surveyed the building in the light of a spluttering gas lamp. A cloud of fog parted just enough for him to see the first floor window. It wasn't barred.

"Can you get up there?" he asked.

"Course," Clarissa said. "I'm a circus star, remember?"

She kicked of her boots, tied the laces together and slug them over her shoulder. Then she unhooked the washing line at both ends and threw that over her shoulder too. "I'll pull you up after," she said.

In one lightning move she sprang onto the top of an outhouse that stood against the wall. Then she shinned up an iron drainpipe, and stepped casually onto the first floor window ledge. "This window's locked from inside an' all. I'll try higher."

Reaching up, she began to climb the wall like a spider, her fingers and toes curled into the gaps between the bricks.

Wild Boy watched in amazement. Sir Oswald had been right – it *was* useful to have an acrobat on his side. He saw that all of the fear had vanished from Clarissa's face, and her eyes seemed to sparkle even in the fog. She looked happy.

She glanced down and saw him watching. "What?" she said.

"Nothing," Wild Boy replied, trying to sound unimpressed. "Hurry it up, will you?"

A few moments later she reached the second floor window. And then she disappeared into the swirling fog above.

Behind Wild Boy, something moved. His heart lurched in his chest, and he flinched back, staring around the yard. "Hello?" he said.

He felt a touch on his shoulder and jumped in fright. But it was just Clarissa's rope. The end was tied in a loop that brushed the ground, waiting for him to climb on. Quickly he stepped into the loop and clung on to the line, as Clarissa began to yank him up the side of the house. As he rose, he looked down, searching the yard for any other movement. But there was none.

The rope scraped over the gutter. "Climb over!" Clarissa called.

Fighting the pain in his shoulder, Wild Boy pulled himself onto a wide ledge that framed a sloping attic roof. Clarissa sat close by, her feet flat against a chimney around which she'd pulled the rope. She was out of breath, but looked pleased with herself.

"This is how we do it in the circus," she said, tugging her boots back on.

The fog was thinning, offering glimpses along the river – the sleek stone arches of London Bridge in one direction, in the other the grim grey bulk of the Tower of London. The fog was confusing, disorientating. It played tricks with your mind. Wild Boy hoped that was what had just happened in the yard...

Clarissa already had her lock picks out as she tried to open a door in the attic roof. She swore, banged a fist against the wood. "This is bolted inside too – this house is like a prison. How could the killer have got in and out?"

Wild Boy wasn't sure, but he was more and more eager to find out. He sensed that the answer could be the clue they needed to catch the killer. But he couldn't solve it unless they could get inside. "Maybe we could—"

CRASH!

With one powerful kick, Clarissa broke open the

door. The crash echoed like thunder around the rooftop. "Got it," she said, grinning.

Wild Boy could barely believe what she'd done. "Are you crazy? The coppers are down there!"

He rushed to the edge of the roof, but was relieved to hear the police still chatting in the street below.

Clarissa pushed the door. "I done my bit," she said. "Now you better do yours."

16

The attic door swung open and the darkness breathed in, sucking thick streams of fog into its gaping mouth.

Wild Boy stepped cautiously into Doctor Griffin's house. It was as dark as a pit. He was supposed to be searching for clues to hunt the killer, but he could barely see five yards in front of his face. He groped his way forward and felt something hard and round perched on a shelf.

"Wait," Clarissa said. "I found a light." She struck the flint and steel of a tinderbox, and lit a candle.

Wild Boy blinked, dazzled. When he looked again he was staring at a human skull. He staggered back and bumped into Clarissa.

"Get off me," she snapped. "Don't—"

Her mouth stayed open but no more words came out. She turned and stared around the low-roofed attic. "*Bones*," she said finally.

The attic was full of bones – hundreds of human bones. There were bones all over the floor, bones in boxes and bones in stacks against the slatted walls. Human skulls lined a shelf, and two whole skeletons guarded the top of a spiral staircase that wound deeper into the house.

"What *is* this place?" Clarissa said.

Wild Boy crouched to examine several books in a pile. Titles on the spines read *Encyclopaedia of Anatomy* and *The Morbid Dissection of the Human Body*. Inside were drawings of human bodies – diagrams of twisting muscles and maps of internal organs, like those he'd seen in Professor Wollstonecraft's caravan.

"I bet the hooded man did this!" Clarissa said. "He must've murdered hundreds of people. He's obsessed with bones!"

"Clarissa," Wild Boy said, before she got carried away, "these bones ain't got nothing to do with the hooded man. This is an anatomy school."

He'd heard of these places – medical schools where doctors carved up corpses to study their insides. Clarissa looked horrified, but Wild Boy felt a shiver of excitement run through his hairs.

Clarissa handed him the candle. "You go first."

The floorboards groaned under his bare feet as he led the way down the rickety spiral of wooden steps. The wallpaper was faded and peeling away, revealing walls that were streaked with damp. There was an acrid smell in the air, like rotting meat, that grew stronger with each step.

At the bottom of the stairs was a room that stretched from window to window along the length of the house. Several wooden tables ran down its centre. On each was a sack filled with something large and lumpy, like a bag of potatoes.

Clarissa pulled her hair around her nose. "Where are we now?"

"A classroom," Wild Boy said.

He spotted signs of the tables' grim purpose everywhere: rags on the floor to soak up sticky spill-ages, iron buckets to catch fatty drippings. This was where the Doctor's students dissected corpses. No wonder the place stank.

His heart beat harder as he guided his candle over the tables and the sacks. Most of the bags were tied with rope, but one had fallen open. Wild Boy raised the top ... and stepped sharply back, gagging with revulsion.

"What is it?" Clarissa said. "What's in there?"

Wild Boy knew he should warn her, but he couldn't resist the opportunity this presented. So he just stepped back and shrugged. "Nothing much," he said.

She had to look. When she did her face turned almost green. Inside the sack was the body of a young woman. With wide open eyes and slate-grey skin, the corpse looked like one of the waxworks that showmen displayed at the fair.

Clarissa leaned against the table, fighting back sick. "You should have said," she seethed.

"I did say."

"You said *nothing much*. There's a dead body in there!"

"A dead body *is* nothing much."

Wild Boy didn't really believe that. Until last week he'd never even seen a corpse. Now he was in a room full of the things. He was scared, but fascinated too.

"Why are they still here?" Clarissa said.

"Must be the fog," Wild Boy said. "The coppers can't take them away till it clears."

His eyes widened as he reached the table at the far end of the room. "Over here," he said. "The murder was done here."

Clarissa rushed closer. "How do you know?"

And then she saw. This table was different to the others. The body laid on it wasn't in a sack but covered by a sheet of black tarpaulin. And painted in white on the sheet were three words:

MURDER DONE HERE

"The Doctor's body," Clarissa said. "It's still here an' all."

Wild Boy raised his candle so it lit the wall behind

the table. There, in crimson letters that had dripped down the wallpaper, was written:

WILD BOY AND CLARISSA DONE IT

Wild Boy hocked up a ball of spit, fired it hard at the wall and watched it trickle down over the bloody writing. Seeing his name written like that – *written in blood* – made him more determined than ever to catch whoever had done this, to make the person pay for setting him up.

He could tell from the look on Clarissa's face that she felt the same. She snorted, and blasted another oyster of phlegm at the wall. "The hooded man's gonna regret messing with us," she said.

Wild Boy turned and took hold of the tarpaulin. "You ready?"

Clarissa nodded. "Ready."

He yanked the sheet from the table, revealing the corpse of Doctor Charles Ignatius Griffin. They both recoiled, revolted by what they saw – the bloated body of a young man with bushy black side whiskers. The man might have been handsome once, but his eyes were now grey and glazed with death, his cheeks were sunken, and the tip of a dark tongue rested between cracked black lips. His sleeves were rolled up, and his shirt and waistcoat were torn and stiff with dry blood.

"It's *him*," Clarissa said.

Wild Boy recognized him too. Doctor Griffin was the man from whom they stole the letter at Greenwich Fair.

Sick rose from Wild Boy's belly and stung his throat. But he forced it back and edged closer. "Look," he said.

On the Doctor's finger was a gold ring, decorated with a single raised letter – a *G*. "Professor Wollstonecraft had the same ring. But it was gone when I saw him in the stable. The killer took it."

Setting his candle down, he pulled the ring from the corpse's rigid finger and slipped it into his pocket.

"You're *stealing* it?" Clarissa said.

"I ain't stealing it. It's a clue."

"Oh. Anyway, how did the killer get in here if all the windows and doors were locked from inside? It doesn't make sense."

"I know…"

"So why are you grinning like that?"

Wild Boy turned, hiding the smile that had spread across his face. Clarissa was right. This crime didn't make sense – and that thrilled him. This was the puzzle he'd come here to solve.

Almost immediately his eyes were drawn to clues around the table. Clarissa kept talking, but he didn't hear. His senses were now totally focused on the crime scene. He stepped back and studied the blood stains on the floor. Then he crouched and picked up an empty sack beside the table. He turned it over, his grin spreading even wider.

"Ha!" he said.

"What? What do you see?"

He rushed to the other end of the table and inspected a cabinet of surgical instruments – long, curving knives and miniature hacksaws. He prodded one of the knives, and then did the same to those in other cabinets along the classroom. His excitement mounted as more clues emerged in the candlelight. He already had a good idea of what had happened here, but a few pieces of the puzzle still didn't fit together.

He rushed back to the Doctor's corpse and examined a large blood stain that ran over the edge of the table's surface. He drew a fingertip slowly around the mark, tracing its pattern.

"Splash marks," he muttered.

Leaning closer, he peeled a single strand of hair from the blood. He held it so close to the candle that its end sizzled in the flame.

"Is that a silver hair, or white?" Clarissa said. Eager to look busy, she grabbed a pencil from a cabinet, and added the clue to her list. "Tell me what you've seen! How did the killer break into the house?"

"He didn't."

"What?"

Wild Boy nodded towards the array of surgical tools. "See them knives? They've been sharpened, but the others in the room ain't."

"So?"

"So the Doctor was about to use them. He was working when he got killed, or he was about to. His sleeves are rolled up, see?"

"He was about to cut up one of these bodies?"

"No. Not one of these."

Wild Boy stood over the empty sack on the floor. In a way, he wished he was wrong about this. In a bigger way, he was exhilarated that he was right. "This bag had a body inside. The Doctor lifted it onto the table. There are threads from the sack on his hand and on the table, see?"

"So what happened to the body?"

"Exactly!" Wild Boy said. "Now look, the Doctor's blood is here on the table. These sides have splash marks. The blood didn't spill out. It *landed* here."

"You mean... What do you mean?"

"I mean he was stabbed while he leaned over the table. Stabbed by someone lying on the table."

"But the person lying on the table... It was the dead body."

"Or so the Doctor thought."

The colour drained from Clarissa's cheeks. "No..." she whispered.

"The killer never broke in, he was *brought* in. He

must have watched this house, known how secure it was. The only people allowed inside that the Doctor didn't know were these corpses. So the killer disguised himself as a dead body – naked, in the sack. He waited until the Doctor lifted the sack onto the table. And just as Doctor Griffin opened it, the killer grabbed his knife and struck."

"But… What sort of person would do that?"

What sort of person *could* do that, Wild Boy wondered. The resolve, the determination. How long had the killer waited in that sack, how patient and still?

He looked up from the table. Clarissa was staring at him. "What?" he said.

"You're grinning again!"

"I… No, I ain't."

"All right," Clarissa said, "so now we know how it was done. But the students who found the Doctor forced their way in as soon as they heard him scream. So the killer was still in this house. Where did he go?"

Wild Boy paced around the table, searching for another clue he'd spotted among the bloodstains. The Doctor's blood was everywhere – dried in splatters about the floor and glistening in the grooves between the boards. Crouching low, he circled one of the stains with his finger. The dark drip tapered away from the murder scene, towards the stairs at the end of the classroom.

"Answer me!" Clarissa demanded. "Where did

he go? The doors were all locked, remember?"

"That way," Wild Boy said. "The killer went downstairs."

"But why?"

Wild Boy felt that tingle again in his hair. He looked up and his emerald eyes twinkled in the candlelight. "I dunno," he said. "But we're about to find out."

17

Wild Boy had no idea what he'd expected to find on the first floor of Doctor Griffin's house, but he hadn't expected *this*.

He raised his candle, scattering glittery light around thousands of glass jars crammed onto shelves and into cabinets up and down the long room. Each jar was filled with golden fluid, and suspended in the fluid was part of a human corpse. Grisly objects loomed from the dark – a severed hand, an amputated foot, the honeycomb lining of a human stomach.

"Looks like a museum," he said, gazing along the rows of pickled organs and limbs.

Clarissa peered anxiously over his shoulder. "It's horrid," she said.

Wild Boy nodded, pretending to agree. In fact, he was fascinated. He wished he had time to look around the Doctor's museum properly, and examine each object in every jar. But he could hear the police officers' voices through a window at one end of the long room, and he knew they could come into this house at any time. He had to focus, find more clues. He was certain the killer had come down here. He'd followed the blood trail from upstairs, and there were more marks on these floorboards.

He moved slowly through the room, crouching with his candle to study the drops of dry blood. What he saw didn't make a lot of sense – the trail led one way and then the other, as if the killer had walked back and forth between the cabinets and shelves. Then it returned to the door and vanished.

Clarissa snatched up one of the jars and gave it a shake. Eyeballs bobbed inside, like tadpoles with sinewy tails. She considered them for a moment, torn between fascination and revulsion. "My father took me to a museum once," she said.

Wild Boy was surprised. It was the first time Clarissa had mentioned her father. He was curious to know more. "What was he like?" he said.

Clarissa considered the question for a moment, staring at the floating eyeballs, but didn't answer. Instead she dumped the jar back onto the shelf, causing the others to knock loudly against one another. "So why did the killer come down here?" she said.

"He was looking for something, but I don't think he found it."

"Why not?"

"He was in a rush. He had to get out the front door before the students came down from upstairs to search the house."

Rising to tiptoes, Wild Boy examined the jars on the shelves up high. Then he crouched and checked those down low. Judging from the thick sheen of dust around their bases, none of them had been moved for months.

"Hey, look at this," Clarissa said.

He hurried to join her at the other end of the room, where a large oil painting hung between the shelves, set in a twisting frame of gilded leaves. The painting showed three smartly dressed men, their faces lit by sparks that flew from some kind of scientific contraption on a table.

Clarissa tapped one of the figures. "Ain't that Professor Wollstonecraft?"

Wild Boy nodded slowly. It was strange to see the old showman dressed so neatly, and without his shaded spectacles. But there was no mistaking that crooked frame and wine-red nose.

"And that man's Doctor Griffin," he said.

"So who's the other bloke?"

The hairs bristled on Wild Boy's back. He recognized the third man, who was taller than the other two, with a thin face, slicked silver hair and a patch over one eye. "That's the man from the fair," he said. "That's the man with the golden eyeball."

"It *is*," Clarissa said. "Look, there's some writing…"

She crouched and read a brass plaque at the base of the frame. *"To Dr Charles Ignatius Griffin. For serving your country as a Gentleman."*

"Gentleman?"

"Says it with a big *G*."

Wild Boy stepped closer, staring at the scientific device in the painting. Sparks flew from a ball of copper tubes fixed to an axle between two wheels.

"A machine…" he said.

Clunk, thunk!

They both turned. The noise had come from downstairs.

"What was that?" Clarissa hissed.

Wild Boy stood still, trying to listen for any other sounds above the thumping of his heart. There were none. He couldn't even hear the police officers out on the street.

"We should go," Clarissa said.

He knew she was right, but he wasn't ready to leave. He felt as if he was close to finding out why the killer had come here. It couldn't just be for this painting. *Think! He had to think!*

"Wild Boy," Clarissa insisted. "The police are just outside that window."

He turned, looked at her. "What did you say?"

"I said we'd better hurry."

"No. You said *window*."

Could it be possible? He looked past Clarissa to the window at the far end of the museum. Then he turned back to the painting, and a grin spread across his hairy face.

"What are you smiling about now?" Clarissa snapped.

"There's no window at this end of the room."

"So?"

"There was outside. You tried to open it, remember?"

"I … I *do*. Where's it gone?"

Wild Boy stepped even closer to the painting. He tried to think like he was back at the fair, picking out clues from the crowd. He let his eyes rove across the surface, let instinct take over… *There!*

"What? What have you seen now?" Clarissa said.

"Look. Up there."

High up, a tiny patch of gilt was missing from the frame. It hadn't been knocked or chipped. It had been worn away, as if something had rubbed against it. Wild Boy reached for the spot, but he was too short. "Feel under there, will you?" he said. "Where the gold's gone."

Clarissa tried to look annoyed at being bossed about, but she couldn't hide her curiosity. Elbowing him aside, she slid her hand under the spot on the frame. Her palm rubbed against the gilded wood. Her eyes widened.

"There *is* something there," she said. "Feels like…"

"A lever?"

"You mean … this painting…?"

"Opens."

Now Clarissa grinned too. "There's a secret room?"

"There's a secret bloomin' room."

18

The painting swung open with a hiss of brown air.

Wild Boy and Clarissa stepped back, horrified by the reek that rushed from within. Whatever was in Doctor Griffin's secret room, it smelled even worse than the classroom upstairs.

The painting creaked on hinges hidden in the frame, and Wild Boy's candlelight fluttered in the stale breeze. "I'll go first," he said.

"Why you?" Clarissa replied. "You ain't braver than me. We'll go together."

They lifted their feet slowly through the frame and set them on creaky floorboards on the other side. The room was long and narrow, with a wooden work-table against one of the brick walls. Fingers of fog tapped at a window, eager to be let in.

Clarissa edged closer to Wild Boy. Her heavy

breaths tickled the hair on his neck.

"Are you scared?" she said.

"I ... I ain't scared of nothing," Wild Boy replied.

"Me neither."

They crept deeper into the thin passage. Several jars from the Doctor's museum sat on the worktable. Except these didn't contain human body parts.

"Animals," Clarissa said.

Wild Boy leaned closer, his eyes wide with fascination. "Not *just* animals," he said.

His candle lit the suspended corpses of a cat, a puppy with its tongue lolling out, a rat shaved of its fur. It looked like the Doctor had experimented on the poor creatures. Thin copper rods stuck from their floating bodies, and wires hung from clips on their limbs. Only one of the animals had been left untouched – a fat eel coiled up and floating in the golden fluid.

Wild Boy tapped the jar curiously. He'd seen an eel like that before.

The eel moved.

Wild Boy lurched back in fright. The candle slipped from his hand, plunging the chamber into darkness.

"What?" Clarissa said. "What is it?"

"It's alive! That thing in the jar!"

Blue light crackled around the room, and Wild Boy remembered where he'd seen a creature like that. Back at the fair, Professor Wollstonecraft had performed tricks with an eel that sparkled when it got angry. An *electrical eel*, he'd called it.

Clarissa gripped his arm. "I can't see!"

"Wait…"

Wild Boy picked up the jar and gave it a shake. The eel bashed its head angrily against the glass. Blue sparks shimmered around its sluggy body, flashing light about the narrow chamber.

"Sorry, slimy," Wild Boy said.

There were more jars along the worktop. In these floated human body parts that had also been used for Doctor Griffin's tests. Metal tubes stuck from the rubbery ventricles of a heart, and silver cogs clung to its fleshy sides. In another jar, a pair of lungs had been grafted with copper wires.

"What is *that*?" Clarissa said.

Beside an empty jar on the work-table sat a small cage made of thin silver bars. Inside the cage was a shrivelled grey ball with a dozen copper wires emerging from its sides. The wires were connected to the bars, so that they held the ball suspended, like a fat spider in the centre of its web. This rotten object was clearly the source of the stench in this chamber. Green puss oozed from its base and dripped to the bottom of the cage.

"What *is* it?" Clarissa said.

Wild Boy leaned closer, wrapping an arm around his nose to mask the smell. He recognized the object from pictures in the Doctor's books. "It's a brain," he said.

Several more books lay beside the cage, but these weren't about anatomy. One was titled *Journal of the Inductive Sciences*. Another was called *Electrical Theory of the Universe*. Inside there were drawings of scientific devices like those that Professor Wollstonecraft had used in his circus show.

"Electricity," Wild Boy muttered.

He picked up a small notebook from among the pile, and shook the eel jar to see the pages. It was crammed with the results of the Doctor's experiments: sketches of bodies and machines, equations and scribbled writing. The words seemed to swirl in the candlelight as a wave of exhaustion washed over Wild Boy. So far all they'd found were more frustrating questions. He wished he could rest and think, far away from the police and the fear of getting caught.

"Are there any clues in that book?" Clarissa said.

"I dunno…"

"What about that worm thing? Is that a clue?"

Wild Boy banged the jar down. "Stop asking so many questions, will you?"

As he spoke, a spark of electricity shot from the eel jar and hit the cage. Clarissa pulled Wild Boy back as a faint blue light crackled around the silver bars, growing brighter. And then – *whoosh!* – the light shot into the cage. Wild Boy and Clarissa watched, amazed, as all of the wires began to glow. Electricity rushed along them and into the brain. For a second the oozing organ shone bright blue, lit from inside. Then it began to twitch, shaking the cage on the table.

And then the light cut out.

Silence. Darkness.

"Let's get out of here," Clarissa said. She rushed back along the chamber and jumped through the open painting.

Wild Boy stuffed the Doctor's notebook in his coat pocket as another crackle of electricity shimmered around the rotten surface of the brain. "What the hell's going on here?" he whispered.

He turned to follow Clarissa, but stopped.

There was a light in the museum.

"Clarissa?" he said.

No reply. The light flickered.

Wild Boy glanced to the window, thinking he should escape while he could. But what about Clarissa? They were in this together now, and he still owed her for saving him at the fair. He couldn't just leave her.

His hands trembled as he edged closer to the hole in the wall. "Who's there?" he called. "If it's you blasted coppers, then you'd better run. Cos I'm a cold-blooded killer and I'm coming out!"

Still no reply. Slowly he stepped into the museum, and immediately he wished he hadn't.

An oil lamp sat on one of the cabinets. The police

were here. An officer lay unconscious and bleeding on the floor between the shelves. A tall cloaked figure stood over him. It was the hooded man. His gloved hand clamped around Clarissa's neck, lifting her several inches from the floor.

He looked up at Wild Boy and dark eyes glinted behind his porcelain mask. "The Wild Boy of London," he said. "You are just in time to watch your friend die."

19

The hooded man's fingers tightened around Clarissa's throat. A bead of sweat dripped from the long bird-like beak of his carnival mask. Clarissa's pale face had turned dark red. She struggled and kicked, but the killer's grip was too strong, crushing the life from her.

"One squeeze," the hooded man said, "and she is gone."

Anger took control of Wild Boy. Before he even knew what he was doing, he leaped over the unconscious police officer and charged at the hooded man, screaming in rage.

But the killer simply raised Clarissa higher. "It is almost as if you wish for it to happen."

"Don't!" Wild Boy cried, stopping and stepping back. "What do you want?"

"You found the Doctor's secret laboratory. There

is something I need from that room."

"Tell me and I'll get it," Wild Boy said. "Just let her go."

"The Doctor's notebook," the hooded man replied. His hand tightened around Clarissa's neck. "You have ten seconds. If you are not back in that time, I will end Miss Everett's life and throw her from that window."

Wild Boy felt the Doctor's journal in his pocket, but stopped himself from bringing it out. He and Clarissa had come here to look for clues to catch the killer. And here he was. Perhaps he could find a way to trap him.

Clarissa's eyes rolled. Her red face began to turn blue. She couldn't register what was happening any more, and Wild Boy was almost glad. He knew she wouldn't like his plan.

"Five seconds," said the hooded man. "Do not think I am joking."

"Wait!" Wild Boy said. "I put it behind you."

The killer's hand eased on Clarissa's neck.

"The book," Wild Boy said. "I hid it so Clarissa wouldn't see it. I was gonna take it and leave her."

The killer's hand tightened again. "I do not believe you."

Wild Boy stared at the shrouded figure, refusing to back down. "Well then, you'll just have to kill her, won't you?"

For a dreadful second he feared that he'd gone

too far. But the hooded man's hand relaxed, and Clarissa gasped a desperate breath. "Which jar?" the killer demanded.

"That one with the eyeballs," Wild Boy said, pointing to the jar that Clarissa had picked up before. "See where the dust's moved at the bottom? I hid the book behind there."

The hooded man moved back, walking with those same awkward, lurching steps that Wild Boy had noticed at the fair. Keeping one hand on Clarissa's neck, the killer reached the other towards the shelf.

"Wait," Wild Boy said. "Just tell me why."

"Why?"

"Why kill those people? Just for some machine?"

And then, from behind the mask came something that caught Wild Boy by surprise – a laugh. A deep, booming laugh so loud it shook the jars on the shelves. "Some machine?" the hooded man said. "No, not just some machine. *The* machine. If you knew what it was, you would think it worth killing for too. You of all people."

"Me? What is it? Tell me!"

The dark eyes narrowed behind the killer's mask. "It is a very powerful machine. It is a machine that changes you. Imagine that, Wild Boy of London. Imagine a machine that could make you normal, like everyone else."

Wild Boy was too stunned to reply. What the killer had said wasn't possible, was it? He could never be normal. No, he couldn't think about that. He had a plan and he had to stick to it. He edged closer, watching the hooded man lift the jar of eyeballs from the shelf.

The killer looked behind the jar. "I am disappointed," he growled. "What exactly did you hope to gain by that charade?"

"*This!*" Wild Boy yelled.

He launched forward and slammed his side against one of the cabinets. The impact sent a bolt of pain up his wounded arm, and a cry roaring from his mouth. But it worked. The cabinet swung down, straight at the hooded man.

20

The cabinet crashed over the hooded man and the killer fell back, letting go of Clarissa. Glass jars smashed on the floor. Stinging vapours swirled into the air, and golden preserving fluid washed across the museum, sloshing with slippery organs.

Wild Boy rushed to Clarissa. He feared that he was too late, but she was breathing – hurt, gasping, but breathing.

She turned, looking groggily around the shattered shelves. "Where is he?" she groaned. "Where did he go?"

The hooded man had gone, but there was no time to worry about him now. The police outside would have heard the crashes.

Wild Boy wrapped an arm around Clarissa's shoulder and helped her stand. They began to shuffle towards the door, but several jars fell from the shelves in front of them. Clarissa screamed and they staggered back, but now more jars shattered to the ground behind. Acid liquid splashed up, soaking Wild Boy's hair and stinging his eyes.

A black shape streaked behind the shelves – the hooded man. Another cabinet toppled over, colliding with the next, falling like dominoes.

Wild Boy gritted his teeth, trying to fight the pain, to think. They had to get out of here but the path to the door was blocked by fallen shelves. They'd have to take their chances with the window.

"This way!" he cried as another cabinet smashed down to their side.

He gripped Clarissa tighter, leading her to the secret room.

"The copper," she said.

Wild Boy looked back and cursed. The police officer still lay unconscious on the floor. One of the shelves could fall on him at any moment.

It ain't your problem, he thought. *Leave him.*

But he knew he couldn't. He swore again, and kept swearing, as he rushed to the officer and dragged him away from the chaos. As he ran back to Clarissa he glimpsed the hooded man dart behind another cabinet, just yards away. He heard Clarissa yell a warning, saw the cabinet swing down…

Wild Boy threw himself to the side, trying to dive out of the way. But he was too late, too slow. He hit the ground and cried out as the cabinet slammed onto him, showering him with glass and body parts. The killer's lamp fell to the floor and set fire to the preserving fluid. A wall of flames roared up around the museum.

Wild Boy tried to move, but his long coat was caught under the shelves. Flames licked across the floor. The hair on his face crackled with heat.

Clarissa staggered to him and tugged his coat, but she was still too weak to tear it free.

"Run!" Wild Boy said. "Get out of here!"

Then another voice spoke. "Give me the book."

The hooded man came closer, walking in those awkward, jerky strides. The tattered leather trail of his cloak caught fire as it swept over the wreckage of the museum. The flames must have scorched his legs but he didn't make a sound as he reached down and took the Doctor's notebook from Wild Boy's pocket.

And then he brought out a knife.

"No!" Clarissa screamed. "Leave him alone!"

With a powerful sweep of his arm, the killer shoved her away.

Dark eyes glinted behind that mask. For a moment, Wild Boy thought he recognized them – he couldn't see their colour, but he knew he had seen them somewhere before.

The killer's knife shone in the firelight as he held the weapon closer.

Wild Boy gritted his teeth, stopping himself

from crying out. If he was going to die, he wouldn't give his murderer the satisfaction of hearing him scream.

But the hooded man didn't kill him. Instead, he swiped the blade and cut Wild Boy's coat from the shelves. Then, in one quick movement, he leaped into the Doctor's secret chamber.

Wild Boy grasped Clarissa's arm as she helped him stand. His wounded shoulder bled onto his coat, his hair was scorched and his lip was bloody. But it wasn't pain he felt – it was anger.

"I never asked for your help!" he yelled at the killer. "I don't owe you nothing!"

The hooded man looked back. The fire lit his white mask blood-red. "Soon, Wild Boy," he said, "you will owe me *everything*."

In a smash and a shower of glass, he jumped through the window.

Wild Boy charged after the killer. The hairs crackled all over his body as he pulled his coat up over his head and burst through the flames. He leaped into the secret chamber and rushed to the broken window, certain that he'd see the hooded man lying injured in the yard below.

"No!" he yelled, slamming his hand against the wall.

The killer was gone. Wild Boy didn't understand – it was twenty feet down. How could he have jumped that without breaking his legs?

"Wild Boy!" Clarissa yelled, climbing into the chamber. "The police!"

More officers appeared in the museum doorway, shielding their faces against the blaze. Through the fire they saw their fallen colleague on the floor, and Wild Boy and Clarissa in the secret room. "It's him!" one of the officers yelled. "It's the Wild Boy of London!"

"It's both of 'em!" another said. "I claim the reward!"

"Go!" Wild Boy cried, urging Clarissa through the window.

She climbed through and jumped. The drop was no problem for her, even onto stone. She landed in a roll, sprang up and set off running down the alley. "Hurry!" she called. "I see the killer!"

"Clarissa, wait!"

Wild Boy clambered out onto the ledge. For a moment he feared he might slip. He pressed himself back against the wall. He wasn't an acrobat – he couldn't jump this.

The police were getting closer.

Jump, he thought. *Jump!*

His coat snapped through the fog as he fell. He landed on top of the outhouse, but his feet plunged through as the shed collapsed. Pain roared from his injured shoulder as he crash-landed in the broken wood.

"There! There! He's down there!"

Policemen's truncheons thwacked onto the ground. Wild Boy rose and staggered to the alley. He saw Clarissa in the distance, and went after her as fast as he could. His side throbbed from the impact of the cabinet, but fear and adrenalin kept him moving as he followed her across the street and into another alley.

And then he stopped.

Clarissa leaned against the alley wall, breathing hard. "I nearly caught him," she said.

The alley ended in a wall that was as high as those on either side. A couple of rats scurried over a pile of crates.

"Where'd he go?" Wild Boy said.

"He came down here," Clarissa said. She kicked one of the crates over, as if she expected to find the killer beneath. All she saw was cobbles. "But he disappeared."

"Wrong alley," Wild Boy said.

"No, it ain't!" Clarissa snapped. "I said he disappeared! Look!"

On the ground beside the crates lay Doctor Griffin's journal, still smoking from the fire. "He must have dropped it," Clarissa said, snatching it up.

That confused Wild Boy even more. The killer had gone to such lengths to steal that book, and… "He *dropped* it?" he said.

"Yeah, and he *disappeared*," said Clarissa, firmly.

She ran to the end of the alley and looked out into the street. "Coppers!"

The police officers stumbled from the Doctor's house, coughing on smoke. One of them saw Clarissa and blasted a shrill warning from his whistle.

"Run!" Wild Boy cried.

He followed her, praying there was another drain they could crawl into, a way back into hiding. But there was none.

Clarissa threw an arm around his back to help him run. But they were too slow. The police were now thirty yards away. Now twenty.

"They're catching up!" Clarissa said. "What do we do?"

And then – a crack, a cry. "Ya!"

Several police officers dived aside as a carriage burst through the fog, jolting over potholes in the road.

"Master Wild! Miss Everett!"

Sir Oswald sat in the driver's perch, the stumps of his thighs tucked under a strap. He lashed the horses harder. "Ha ha! Old Ozzie's got your backs!"

Clarissa leaped onto the footplate and swung open the door. She leaned from the carriage as it clattered forward, calling to Wild Boy. "Gimme your hand!"

One of the policemen charged up behind Wild Boy and tried to grab his coat, but Wild Boy gripped Clarissa's hand and she hauled him up into the carriage. Sir Oswald thrashed the reins and they raced away along the street.

Wild Boy tumbled into the footwell beneath the seats, breathing hard. Clarissa glared down at him. Her face was bruised, her coat was burned and speckled with broken glass, and her eyes were raw from the preserving fluid. She dropped Doctor Griffin's journal to the carriage floor.

"I hope this was worth it," she said.

21

They rode east through the waking city as the last wisps of fog peeled from the houses and dawn blazed across the sky, scattering the cobbles with gold. Tired-looking figures emerged from doorways, buttoning waistcoats and stretching stiff limbs. Some of them stopped to watch a poster-boy plaster new signs to a wall, demanding the capture of the Wild Boy of London and the Fairground Fiend Clarissa Everett. The price on their heads had risen.

Wild Boy curled up tighter in the carriage footwell. He didn't know where he was headed and he didn't especially care. For now, he was happy to let Sir Oswald carry them to safety. Everything hurt – his shoulder, his side, his jaw, his teeth. Each time the carriage rattled over a pothole it felt like someone was punching his head.

Clarissa lay across the carriage seats, her coat draped over her like a blanket. The hooded man's attack had left a sunset of bruises across her face. Wild Boy kept thinking how close she'd come to death. Just seconds away, the squeeze of a hand...

And for what?

Doctor Griffin's journal sat beside him in the footwell. He knew there would be clues in it to help catch the killer, but he couldn't bring himself to look. He wanted a few minutes to close his eyes, to think about anything else. But it was impossible. His mind was now occupied by just one thing – what the killer had said at the Doctor's house.

"*The machine what changes you*," Wild Boy whispered.

The hooded man had claimed the machine could make him normal, like everybody else. Could such a device really exist?

The carriage shuddered to a stop.

"We are here," Sir Oswald said as he swung from the driver's perch. "It is safe for now. But hurry."

Wild Boy slid across the footwell and poked his head from the door. They'd arrived near the river, where a rickety wharf buzzed with the activity of a market. Grizzled watermen hauled barrels of brandy and crates of fish from decks to dock. They were much too busy to notice this carriage parked at the far side of the wharf.

A gust of wind swished off the river but that

wasn't why Wild Boy shivered. He climbed from the carriage and stared at a dark building that rose beyond the wharf. It was a miserable building, abandoned and left to rot by the riverside. Every window was smashed and crows perched like gargoyles on their crumbling ledges.

For a moment Wild Boy forgot all about being seen. He didn't even notice the racket of the market, or the sewagey reek of the river. Right then the only thing in his world was that building.

A drum began to beat inside him. He whirled around and yelled at Sir Oswald. "Why did you bring us *here*?"

A shadow fell across Sir Oswald's face. "The circus and showmen are camped in a warehouse on the other side of the wharf," he said. "This building is deserted. It seemed like a good place to hide."

"No! You don't know what this place is."

"I do, Master Wild. And I know how you must feel. But you cannot stay outside any longer. It is too dangerous."

He was right, Wild Boy knew. They were lucky they'd not been noticed already. Part of him felt that he'd rather be caught than hide in *there*. But after all he'd been through, he couldn't just give up. He pulled his coat tighter around him and led the way to the dark building.

Clarissa climbed from the carriage, watching curiously. "Sir Oswald?" she said. "What is that place?"

"My dear, that is the workhouse where Master Wild grew up."

The workhouse. *His* workhouse.

As he looked up at the ugly block of bricks, Wild Boy's insides twisted with dread. He leaned against the wall, trying to fight back the painful memories that flooded his mind. But it was no use, there were too many. This was the place where he'd been abandoned as a baby, where he'd spent eight miserable years until Augustus Finch had taken him away.

It was a coincidence, he knew. The fair had camped in a warehouse near the docks while they prepared for Bartholomew Fair in the City. But still, he felt as if the building had dragged him back, to remind him of what he was.

As if he could ever forget.

He climbed through one of the broken windows and gazed around the empty brick shell. The building was derelict, but it hadn't been much more cheerful when he'd lived here – the same bare walls, the same bleak cold. Only the table had disappeared, and the stench of rotten food was now replaced by a powerful reek of damp and stale urine.

Clarissa clambered inside and glanced anxiously around the room, as if she half expected someone to leap from the musty darkness. Seeing that they were alone, she looked at Wild Boy and bit her lip. "Is it true?" she asked softly. "That you lived here?"

"This was the dining hall," Wild Boy said. "Where the other boys ate."

"Not you though?"

"No. Not me."

He walked out of the hall and up the stairs. With each creak in the floorboards he remembered another beating from Master Bledlow. He could almost hear the chants of the other boys echoing around the mouldering walls – *Mon-ster! Mon-ster!* At the top of the stairs, the door still bore that mocking charcoal sign. *WILD ANIMAL! BEWARE!*

He breathed in deeply, trying to fight the emotions that were overwhelming him. *Don't cry*, he told himself. *Don't you dare cry.* He'd spent eight years here refusing to cry, never giving them the satisfaction. He was desperate not to now.

He pushed the door open and stepped inside. Memories hit him like a punch to the stomach, knocking the breath from his body. He gripped the door as his legs buckled.

"No!" he gasped. "Please … don't…"

But he couldn't help it. He slumped to the floor as tears stung his eyes and soaked into the hairs on his face. He'd tried so hard not to feel sorry for himself, to always act tough. But there had been times in this room when he'd felt so lonely he'd thought he might die. He remembered sitting in the dark listening to the other boys laughing, and how all he wanted in the world was a friend. But he'd known they were laughing at him. Every single person in this building had hated him because of how he looked. And, now, every person in the city did too.

Something moved.

He looked up, wiping tears and snot from his face. A crow sat on the window ledge, watching him through the broken glass with unblinking eyes. Its loud *caw* rang around the room like a shriek of laughter. Wild Boy remembered how it seemed that even the birds used to mock his misery.

The crow flapped away as Wild Boy picked himself up and stepped to the window. Outside was still the same view – a sliver of street in one direction, the river in the other and the busy docks below. *His* view.

The floorboards creaked. Wild Boy turned, his hands tightening into fists. Suddenly he was that eight-year-old boy again, terrified of whoever came into this room.

But it was only Sir Oswald, sitting in the doorway on the stumps of his missing legs. He removed his hat and smoothed back his salt-and-pepper hair, as if he was visiting a grieving widow. "I am sorry, Master Wild," he said. "This was the only safe place I could think to keep you."

"What happened to it?" Wild Boy asked.

Sir Oswald came closer, his upper body swinging between his arms. "I made some enquiries. The workhouse closed down over a year ago. The master in charge met with an accident."

"Accident?"

"He fell into the river. Drowned."

Wild Boy turned. He hated Master Bledlow, and had dreamed for three years of getting revenge on him. But he'd never wished him dead. He felt deflated, empty.

"The other boys," Sir Oswald said, "were mostly placed in families or on apprenticeships."

"Lucky them," Wild Boy muttered.

He remembered all the visitors who had come to this room, and how his heart had surged with the hope that they would take him away. But they never had – they'd just paid Bledlow to see the freak. And then that night, the night the showman came. Wild Boy had thought that, finally, he was embarking on some sort of new life. But nothing had really changed – the bullies had just got more dangerous.

"Master Wild," Sir Oswald said. "I am sure that you have nothing but dark memories of this place. But think of it like this – without it you would never have developed your skill."

"Skill?"

"The way you see things…"

"It's just looking, Sir Oswald."

"Well then, no one else can look the way you do. It is a rare talent, Master Wild, whether you accept it or not. You must use it to save yourself and Miss Everett. She tells me that the killer is still after some sort of machine, something to do with electricity."

Wild Boy considered his reflection in the broken window, a monstrous mess of tangled hair, filth from the sewers, blood and dried preserving fluid. Even his eyes had lost their sparkle. "Sir Oswald," he said. "The killer said the machine can change a person, change how they look. Do you think that's true?"

Sir Oswald thought about this for a moment. "I am hardly an expert on such matters, Master Wild. But I once spoke with Professor Wollstonecraft about electricity. He told me that it was an extraordinary power, capable of incredible things. So, yes, perhaps it is possible. But I know this: you must keep going. Find this machine and perhaps you will find the killer. Do not give up now, Master Wild. If you do, then they have won. Mr Finch, Master Bledlow, and all those boys who persecuted you here... They will all have won."

He shoved his hat back on his head. "Now, speaking of Mr Finch, I must return to the warehouse."

Finch. Wild Boy had almost forgotten about him. It seemed strange that only a few days ago his biggest worry had been a beating from the showman. He felt sorry for Sir Oswald – without a show Finch would probably be drunk all day.

"I will return in an hour with food and clean clothes," Sir Oswald said. "Promise me you will not go anywhere until I return?"

Wild Boy managed another slight smile. "Where else am I gonna go?"

The grin returned to Sir Oswald's wrinkled face. "That's the spirit! Miss Everett has lit a fire downstairs, so I suggest you make yourself at home. Quite industrious, that young lady. I knew the two of you would make a fine team. Keep looking, Master Wild. It is not over yet."

Sir Oswald raised his hat in salute, and left.

Wild Boy turned back to the window. He knew Sir Oswald was right. He *had* learned his skill here – if it was a skill. Perhaps he could save himself, and Clarissa. But what then? He'd still be a freak. Nothing would have changed. Unless…

Unless it *was* true.

"The machine what changes you," he whispered.

22

Downstairs in the dining hall, Clarissa sat beside a fire that smouldered in a square of bricks. Her bruises had darkened into a storm that raged down the side of her freckled face. A spot of blood seeped through the bandage she'd wrapped around her forehead. With a scrap of cloth, she scrubbed dirt from the sequins of her dress.

"You angry again?" she said, without looking up.

"No," Wild Boy replied. "I'm tired."

"Me too."

He sat down beside her and pulled his coat around himself to let the fire dry it out. "You all right then?" he asked.

Clarissa shrugged, touched her bruised neck. She wasn't all right, Wild Boy knew that, but she wasn't going to say so. Acting tough, that was how you got by in their world. Acting tough even if you were screaming inside.

They sat in silence for a while. It didn't feel like awkward silence – they were both just pleased to rest and get warm. For the first time, Wild Boy realized that he was glad to have Clarissa there. But he could see how upset she was, how fragile she seemed all of a sudden. It was as if the hooded man's attack had shattered her confidence. He tried to think of something he could say to make her feel better, but in the end it was Clarissa who broke the silence.

"Do you really think we'll catch him?" she said.

"Course we will," Wild Boy replied, sounding more sure than he felt.

"But you saw how tough he is," Clarissa said. "He hardly even felt that fire on his legs."

"He ain't as tough as us. We're fairgrounders, remember? You're a circus star."

"I know. Only … only maybe the circus ain't so great as I say."

Wild Boy poked the fire, and sparks crackled into the dark. He realized that it had felt good talking to Sir Oswald about his past. Maybe Clarissa needed to talk about hers too. "Why's your mother so angry at you?" he said.

Clarissa rubbed harder at her sequins. "Because I remind her of my father. Funny thing is, I look like *her*. I mean, how she used to look before he ran away. She was beautiful, you know. And the circus used to be nice too. But now she only hires crooks and thugs. The show ain't fun no more neither, not like it was. The animals are too thin, the clowns are always drunk and fighting. I seen people walk away from it crying, not laughing."

"Were you going to run away an' all?"

"I dunno what I'd have done. Dunno what I'll do now, even if we do catch the hooded man. What about you?"

Again Wild Boy thought about the machine. "I dunno either," he said. "I reckon we'll work it out."

"We ain't enemies no more, are we?"

"No. Not no more."

"I didn't think so. We ain't so different really." She stopped scrubbing her dress and looked at him, considering the hair on his face. Grinning, she reached and brushed some dirt from the hairs on his cheek. "Only, you could be cleaner. Do you *ever* wash?"

Wild Boy was surprised that he didn't flinch back. In fact, he didn't mind her touching him. But he pushed her hand away, pretending to be annoyed. "Leave off, will you."

"But your hair is so filthy. I use oil on mine, so it's shiny. Look, see?"

"Yeah, I see!"

"You smell dirty too – you did even before the sewers."

Wild Boy touched the hair on his face. He'd never really tried to look nice. He'd always thought it wasn't possible for someone like him. But he shook the idea away. "Ain't we meant to be talking about the killer? Let's see that list again."

"My list!" Clarissa said.

Wild Boy shuffled closer, and they studied the paper in the firelight.

Clues so far
- Killer walks funny
- Killer knew the Professor
- Marks in mud by Professor's body – from a cane?
- Marks on killer's hood – lives in place with low ceiling
- Hair by Doctor's body – silver or white?

Clarissa tapped her pencil against the page. "We need to add the new ones," she said. "I couldn't hear what the hooded man said at the house. Did he tell you anything useful?"

"What about?"

"This machine he's after."

"No," Wild Boy said quickly. "He didn't say nothing about it."

She looked at him curiously, and immediately he felt bad. He didn't know why he'd lied to her. He still thought that what the killer had said sounded ridiculous. But if it *was* true…

The truth was, he didn't want Clarissa knowing how interested he was becoming in this machine. They were meant to be finding the killer, after all.

"So what should we add?" Clarissa asked.

Wild Boy thought for a moment, replaying the scenes from the Doctor's house over in his mind and picking out the important details. "Well, the killer can jump. That drop from the window was high. Most people would break their legs."

"I jumped it easily."

"But you're an acrobat."

Clarissa added the fact to her list. "And he can disappear," she said.

"Eh?"

"In the alley."

"He didn't disappear. He just made it look that way."

"You mean a trick?"

"What was in the alley?" Wild Boy asked.

"Boxes. The walls. Oh, and some rats. Maybe he turned into a rat." Clarissa examined the list, as if all the answers they needed were there. "The killer is the man with the golden eyeball," she decided. "He's the only one in the Doctor's painting that ain't dead, and he had the same ring as him and the Professor.

There's that hair an' all and the cane marks by the Doctor's body."

"I only said they *looked* like cane marks."

"What else could they be? Hobnail boots maybe?"

"Maybe," Wild Boy agreed. He felt more alert every second they spoke about the investigation. It was as if the misery of this workhouse, that heavy black shroud, had lifted away. His thoughts became clear and focused.

There was one big clue that they'd not yet considered. "Here, give us the Doctor's notebook," he said.

"Don't get so close," Clarissa said.

"I wasn't!"

"You just did."

"Just give us the book, will you?"

"Here," she said. "Lucky for us the killer dropped it."

Wild Boy wasn't sure it had been luck. But he could think of only one other reason why the killer would have left the book – he didn't need it any more. The hooded man had already seen what he needed to see.

The hairs prickled all over his body as he opened the book. Most of the pages were charred from the flames, but he could still read some of the Doctor's writing. The notes seemed to be the results of experiments. He flicked through and read the entries.

Prisoner Thomas Weems – A dismal trial upon this subject, who lasted not five seconds under the machine's full charge. Minimal response in his frontal cerebral lobe.

"The machine," Wild Boy whispered. He kept flicking.

Prisoner Arthur Doyle – The subject's brain proved highly responsive to the increase in charge. His heart, however, was quite unequal to the challenge. Another failure. Tomorrow we try again.

Prisoner Henry Mayhew – Yet another failure! Professor Wollstonecraft may know electricity, but I know the human body. To have any hope of success we must increase the charge!

Prisoner Clarence Rook – The machine works! The subject underwent complete physical change! What a fool Wollstonecraft is to have left the Gentlemen just as we are on the verge of success! But we must test it again. We must be sure.

"Look," Clarissa said. "One of the pages is missing."

Wild Boy held the book nearer to the fire and examined the line where the paper had been ripped out near the back. The next page was blank. "It's a clean tear," he said. "No smoke stains. The page got torn *after* the book was burned."

"*I* didn't tear it out!" Clarissa said.

"No, the killer did. There must've been something important on that page, some clue to finding the machine."

"Great," Clarissa muttered. "So the book's useless now."

"Nah," Wild Boy said, getting an idea. "We just gotta look harder."

He tugged his coat sleeve over his hand and plucked a smouldering stick from the side of the fire. Clarissa slid closer as he ran the charred end of the stick gently over the blank page at the back of the book. As the paper darkened they could just make out faint impressions from the Doctor's pencil on the missing page. All they could see were a few words that had been written harder than the others. Wild Boy recognized the first two immediately.

The machine

"Amazing," Clarissa said.

Wild Boy felt a strange feeling right then, a warm glow inside. It took him a few moments to realize that it was pride. He was pleased to have impressed her. But he tried not to think about it as he rubbed the paper, teasing more words from the darkness.

"That word looks like *burned*," Clarissa said.

"There's another two here."

Wild Boy held the page closer to the fire and read the ghost writing. "Looks like a name. *Mary Somerset*."

Clarissa snatched the book, checked it herself. "Mary Somerset?"

"You know who that is?" Wild Boy said. "Maybe if we find her, we'll find the machine, and then the killer an' all."

A smile flashed across Clarissa's bruised face. She *did* know, he could tell, but she wasn't going to say just yet. Her knees clicked as she rose from the fireside. "Well, don't just sit there," she said, dropping the book in Wild Boy's lap. "We got a killer to catch."

She crossed to the workhouse window, and leaped into the night.

"Bloomin' cow," Wild Boy muttered. But a wide grin broke across his face too, and a familiar tingle ran through his hairs. *Mary Somerset*. Somehow Clarissa knew that name. The hunt for the hooded man – and for the machine – was back on.

23

The full moon shone through cracks in the dirty clouds, dappling the docks with light. A stray cat bolted behind a heap of nets, but otherwise the wharf was empty. Boats creaked eerily against their tethers.

Heart pounding, Wild Boy raced after Clarissa, weaving between stacks of crates, darting around a mound of slimy nets and then hiding behind a cart that was filled with props from the circus. "Hey," he whispered. "What are we doing here?"

Clarissa ignored him as she searched for something in the cart. A trombone fell from the side, and Wild Boy just managed to catch it before it clattered to the ground.

He swore at her, but she wasn't listening. She hadn't even told him what she was looking for – *"Something we need,"* was all she'd say – and he wasn't asking again. He knew she wouldn't tell him, just as she'd not said how she knew Mary Somerset, that name in Doctor Griffin's book. She enjoyed being in charge.

Wild Boy leaned around the side of the cart, checking that they hadn't been seen. From here he could see straight into the iron-roofed warehouse where the travelling fair had camped. Everyone was there – the showmen, the circus crew, the performers and stall holders – all making last-minute preparations before riding to Bartholomew Fair in the heart of London.

And there, among the vans, was his old freak show. Sir Oswald was still fixing up the caravan, hanging on to the side with one arm as he connected a new pipe to those that already snaked around the wooden walls.

Augustus Finch leaned against the van. The scars were shiny across the showman's face, and his badger-streak hair hung wild about his eyes. He still struggled to stand on his wounded foot, which pleased Wild Boy to see.

"Serves the old goat right," he muttered.

He realized that he wasn't scared of Finch any more. So much had happened since he'd fled that caravan. He had bigger fears to face now.

Clarissa came up beside him. She was looking into the warehouse too, and she had seen her mother.

Mary Everett looked even more frightening than Finch, with fresh white make-up smeared across her face and staining her greasy red hair. The powder crumbled from her cheeks as she leaned on her crutch and roared orders at a couple of porters fixing a wagon wheel.

"Let's go," Clarissa said.

Wild Boy grabbed her arm. He had to say something. Clarissa still had a chance to get out of this. Her mother might beat her, but bruises and broken bones heal. "Clarissa," he said, "you don't have to run. The circus will hide you if you go back. Your mother would—"

"She ain't my mother," Clarissa said. "Least, not no more. I'll never go back."

She slung a sack over her shoulder, stuffed with a few items she'd stolen from the cart. "We waiting for Sir Oswald?" she asked.

Wild Boy couldn't help feeling relieved. He didn't want to go on alone. But from now on, it was just him and Clarissa. He didn't know where they were headed, only that it would be dangerous. Sir Oswald had risked enough to help them already. "It's just us," he said.

They looked at each other for a moment. Neither spoke, and neither smiled. Wild Boy wanted to do both. He opened his mouth to say something, but Clarissa sprang up and set off towards the street at the end of the wharf. "Mary Somerset," she called, "this way!"

"Won't we be seen?" Wild Boy said.

She'd been waiting for that question. She rustled in her sack and brought out a pair of purple clown shoes and a single lump of coal. Her eyes twinkled in the moonlight.

"I got a plan," she said.

"Run for your lives, it's the Wild Boy of London!"

Wild Boy waddled uneasily along the cobbled street, placing each step carefully to avoid tripping over the elongated clown shoes. If he hadn't been so scared he'd have felt ridiculous.

But he had to admit this was a good plan. There must have been a hundred people staring at him right then, and all they could see of him were his green eyes staring through holes in the sack. Across the front, Clarissa had scrawled a monstrous charcoal face with jagged fangs and the words *WILD BOY* sootily beneath. She wasn't wearing much of a disguise herself – just a cloth cap to hide her flame-coloured hair.

"Run for your lives!" she yelled. "The Wild Boy of London will eat you up!"

They were crossing London Bridge, headed for the north bank of the city. Workers chiselled blocks of stone under the glare of the gas lamps that lined the parapets, repairing the bridge. Around them the night rang with the clip-clops of horses and cries of costermongers selling rat poison, razor blades, garter clips and grease remover.

Most people were too busy to care about a boy

in costume, but one of the stone cutters swaggered over and blew a kiss at Wild Boy's sack face.

"Haw, haw!" he guffawed. "The Wild Boy's a softy! I thought he growled like a wolf."

Clarissa's fingers dug into Wild Boy's arm. "Hear them, Wild Boy of London? *Growl.*"

"Grrr," Wild Boy said.

"Growl *louder*!"

"I said *grrr*, didn't I?"

He knew she was enjoying this – not just his disguise, but being in charge. Whoever Mary Somerset was, he hoped she was close. He wasn't used to wearing any shoes at all, let alone clumsy clown boots like these.

A stone hit Wild Boy from behind. A gang of boys sat on the edge of the bridge, throwing rubble at passers by. One of them spotted him and raced over, determined to look under his sack.

Wild Boy tried to stay calm, to fight his fear and to think. He stepped back, ready to attack. He'd kick the boy in the face, he decided, and hope no one saw the hairy foot that shot from under his disguise.

But just as he came close, Clarissa snatched the boy's arm.

"Can you swim?" she asked him.

"Eh?" the boy grunted. "Why'd you wanna know that?"

"Because if you touch my friend, I'll throw you in the river."

They eyeballed each other – a battle of wills. The boy was from the streets, but Clarissa was tougher, and he could tell. She let go of his arm, and he turned and scampered away.

Clarissa burst out laughing. "Did you see that?"

"Clarissa," Wild Boy said. "Look!"

The boy had run back to his friends. He pointed at Clarissa, and the whole gang leaped from the parapet and barged their way closer.

The smile slipped from Clarissa's face. "Can we fight that many?" she said.

"I'm in a sack, remember? We gotta get out of here."

"Hold my arm!"

Wild Boy gripped her tightly as she led him through the crowds. They reached the end of the bridge and she pulled him into a side street, away from the danger of the gang. "They're gone," she said, sighing in relief. "This is the way anyway. Come on."

They entered a maze of dark lanes and courtyards. Shabby buildings scowled at them as they passed. Wild Boy heard steamboat bells close by on the Thames. Even through the sack, he could smell the river's turgid water.

He wasn't surprised that Clarissa knew her way around here. They weren't far from West Smithfield, where Bartholomew Fair was held each year. He guessed that she used to sneak from the fairground and explore these streets, and found himself wishing he'd known her better back then. He'd never really thought he could be friends with anyone. But maybe he'd been wrong.

"All right," Clarissa said, "we're here."

Wild Boy peered eagerly through the holes in the sack. They had stopped in the middle of a particularly squalid street near the riverbank. On one side stood rickety wooden houses. On the other was a decrepit stone church with a wild, overgrown graveyard. A crooked gas lamp cast a queasy glow over its rusty iron gate.

"Mary Somerset," Clarissa said.

"Where?"

She turned him around, so his gaze fell again on the church. "There."

Wild Boy stared up at the church's tower as a bat dipped in and out of the moonlight. Finally he understood. "*Saint* Mary Somerset," he said.

It wasn't a person. It was a church.

24

The graveyard gates were twelve feet tall, wet with rain and armed at the top with razor-sharp spikes. Clarissa was up and over them in seconds – a jump, a flip and a perfect landing on the other side. She grinned at Wild Boy between the bars.

"Bet you can't get through."

Wild Boy checked again that the street was empty, and then tugged off his sack disguise and kicked his clown shoes into a puddle. He brushed back the hair on his face, and grinned at Clarissa. "Bet I can," he said.

Pulling the gate on its chain, he stepped sideways through the gap. Clarissa muttered something about cheating, but he pretended not to hear as he peered through the misty moonlight at St Mary Somerset church. The building, once perhaps beautiful, was now almost completely blackened by grime. The only signs of its original colour were four pinnacles of white stone that rose from the top of the tower, like skeleton fingers reaching into the night.

Clarissa peered warily around the dark grave-yard. "Do you think the killer's here?"

Wild Boy crouched and examined the gravel path that led to the church. He couldn't see any signs of footprints, or other clues to suggest anyone had been here since it had last rained. But he was sure this church was important. He brought the Doctor's notebook from his pocket and reread the words from the torn-out page. *The machine ... burned ... Mary Somerset.*

"The machine what changes you," he said.

"What?" Clarissa said.

"Nothing."

Clarissa trudged to a wooden hut off the path, unlocked the door with her picks and stole a lantern she saw inside. She struck the flint, and handed Wild Boy the light. Now that she'd led them here, she was happy to let him take charge. "So what are we looking for?"

Wild Boy wished he had an answer. His big eyes searched the outside of the church for clues to make sense of the words in the Doctor's book. The building was derelict, but it didn't look like it had suffered any fires recently. Nor did any of these gravestones, or the —

He closed his eyes and groaned. What an idiot

he'd been! "Of course!" he said. "The graves."

That middle word in the book wasn't *burned*.

It was *buried*.

"We gotta check them graves," he said.

They set off through the graveyard that ran along the side of the church. Mouldering headstones rose at odd angles from long, straggly grass. Wild Boy's lantern cast a shaky glow over ivy-covered head-stones, broken-faced angels and sacred promises carved in stone – *We will never forget you… I will fear no evil… I will rise again…*

He had never been in a graveyard before, and he didn't like it. He thought he saw something move behind one of the stone tombs. He turned, but there was no one there – just the wind rustling the long grass.

"Over here!" Clarissa called.

He rushed to where she stood beneath the sprawling arms of a yew tree. The grass here reached halfway up his legs, and the headstones – small and cheaply cut – were stained with patches of glisten-ing slime.

Wild Boy held the lantern over one of the graves. At the top of the headstone, he could just see a faint letter scratched beneath the mould.

"Another *G*," Clarissa said. "It's them again, the Gentlemen."

Wild Boy rubbed away a patch of the mould to reveal the name on the headstone.

"Never heard of him," Clarissa said.

Yes, you have, Wild Boy thought. She just didn't remember. He opened the Doctor's notebook and flicked to the page. "Here. This is him…"

Prisoner Thomas Weems — A dismal trial upon this subject, who lasted not five seconds under the machine's full charge…

His heart began to beat faster – not fear this time, but excitement. "Let's check these other graves," he said.

They ran through the long grass, inspecting names on the stones under the yew. "Rook," Clarissa said. "This one says Clarence Rook. That name's in the Doctor's book, ain't it? This stone's got a *G* on it an' all."

"And these two," Wild Boy said. "Doyle and Mayhew."

He crouched to examine another grave, but Clarissa closed the shutter on the lantern. "There's a carriage," she whispered.

Wild Boy followed her gaze towards the street. The carriage was big and black with a golden emblem on the door. Its light rippled a crimson glow across puddles as it rattled closer. It was slowing down.

"We should hide," Clarissa said.

They rushed behind the trunk of the yew, and watched the carriage come to a stop outside the gates. Wild Boy could now see the emblem on the door – it was a golden letter G.

The door opened and four men emerged, dressed in frock coats and stovepipe hats. As the tallest man stepped into the lamplight, a glint of gold shone from under the shadow of his hat.

"That's him," Wild Boy said. "That's the golden-eyed man."

The other men slid a long wooden crate from inside the carriage. Grunting with effort, they carried it towards the gates.

The golden-eyed man unlocked the gates. "Hurry, Gentlemen," he said.

Wild Boy and Clarissa huddled together, barely daring to breathe, as two of the men carried the crate past the yew tree. The golden-eyed man followed – one hand leaning on his cane, the other raising a lantern against the dark. Then he stopped, just yards from the yew tree. His one good eye narrowed as it scanned the graveyard. He gripped the top of his cane, and – *swish* – drew a long steel blade from inside.

Wild Boy's hands clenched into fists. He and Clarissa had made it this far, and he wasn't going to let this man catch them now. Not now.

The golden-eyed man stepped towards the tree.

Clarissa gripped Wild Boy's arm. She was shaking, but he could see in her eyes that she too was ready to fight.

The golden-eyed man came closer.

"Sir!" a voice called.

The third man ran along the path from the gates, clutching something he'd found. He opened his mouth to speak, but the golden-eyed man silenced him with a look.

"May I remind you, Mr Beauchamp, that we are a *secret* organization."

"Sir?" the other man said.

"Perhaps you might lower your voice."

"I'm sorry, sir," the man whispered. "I found this."

Wild Boy could see what the man held – it was the sack that Clarissa had made him as a disguise.

The golden-eyed man slid his sword back into his cane. He held the sack to his lantern and studied its Jack-o'-lantern face and charcoal writing. Just for a second he seemed to wince. Wild Boy remembered the agony he'd seen the man in at the fair, and the relieving liquid he kept in his false eye.

But the man stopped himself from reaching for it. His jaw clenched, and he handed the sack back to his companion.

"It is the boy," he said.

"Impossible, sir!"

"It *is* the boy. And he was not alone."

"The circus girl?"

"Presumably." The golden-eyed man was silent for a moment. "We have underestimated those two," he said finally. "Perhaps quite seriously."

"Sir, this is grave news. If those two learn about—"

"I am aware of the gravity of our situation, Mr Beauchamp. That is why I wish you to stop speaking. There remains a killer on the loose, and I can assure you that it is neither Wild Boy nor Clarissa Everett. Whoever it is, he is after the machine. And that means he is after us. But for now this crate remains our priority."

He moved away from the yew, towards the church, where he unlocked the doors and pushed them open. He followed his companions as they carried the crate inside.

"We shall take care of the children later," he said.

The doors closed with a hollow *thud*.

Immediately Wild Boy burst from behind the tree and ran for the church, weaving between headstones and tangles of bramble. That man had said he had the machine – Wild Boy had to know if it was real, if there really was a machine that could change how he looked. But as he neared the doors, another *thud* echoed around the graveyard. It came from the church.

The blackened walls had begun to shake. And then a louder noise echoed from inside – rattling chains and a deep, grinding sound, like stone scraping against stone. The glass rattled in the broken windows.

And then silence.

"What just happened?" Clarissa said, catching up.

Wild Boy had no idea, but he was desperate to find out. He looked to a large broken window, about thirty feet high. "Can you get up there to see?"

Clarissa hesitated, touching the bruise on her face. But she nodded, and began to climb. Wild Boy barely saw how she managed it – she was up in seconds, clinging to the window ledge and peeking through one of the remaining stained glass panels.

"What can you see?" Wild Boy whispered.

"Wait there," she replied.

She climbed higher, and then – in one quick move – swung feet-first through the empty part of the window.

"Clarissa!" Wild Boy called.

He didn't hear her land. The only sounds were the krekking of a crow high on the tower, and the whistle of wind through the broken window.

And then the door creaked slowly open.

Wild Boy staggered back, fists trembling. But it was just Clarissa. The sequins on her dress shone red and gold in the light from inside the church.

"You won't believe this," she said.

Cautiously, Wild Boy stepped through the door. He brushed hair away from his eyes, and stared.

A fallen statue of an angel lay shattered across the aisle between rows of wooden pews. Above it, a candle flickered on a stand, its light glimmering off a bronze cross that stood in the centre of the altar. But otherwise the church was empty.

The men had vanished.

25

"It don't make sense," Clarissa said. "Where did they go?"

She plucked the candle from its stand and waved the light behind one of the church pews, as if she might find the golden-eyed man and his companions hiding there. Out of ideas, she glared angrily at Wild Boy.

"They're getting away!" she said. "You must have seen *something*."

Wild Boy had seen plenty. As he'd watched the men in the graveyard, his eyes had sought out clues on shirt cuffs, trouser knees and shoe heels. Three of them had served in the army, and one had been in the navy. All of them had walked through a stone tunnel that day, three had played billiards and the golden-eyed man had won. But none of that explained where they had gone. They had locked the church door, lit a candle and then disappeared.

"Anyway," Clarissa said. "This proves the golden-eyed man is the killer. The hooded man disappeared an' all, remember, in that alley."

Wild Boy ignored her, trying to think. There was another door to the side of the altar, but it was bolted from inside. And besides, why would the men have come through the front door just to leave by the back? He remembered the noises – the rattling chains and scraping stone.

Clarissa muttered something else, but her voice faded into a drone as he turned slowly around. He didn't know what he was looking for, only that he'd realize when he saw it. Suddenly his eyes were moving with incredible speed, shooting around the church. He saw a tear in a tapestry, a crack in a stone memorial, the worn-down face of a wooden cherub...

And Clarissa's candle.

"Don't move," he said.

Clarissa froze. "What? What is it?"

"That flame is flicking."

"Is that all?" she said, relieved. "Course it is, the window's broken."

"No. It's flicking the other way."

Clarissa considered the light curiously. Wild Boy was right – the flame was rippling gently *towards* the window. The draught was coming from the other direction.

Wild Boy rushed up the aisle. His senses were now on high alert, his mind working faster than ever. He rolled up his coat sleeve and held his forearm close to the candle. The long hair on his wrist swayed in a breeze from below. They fluttered harder as he held his arm near the base of the stone altar.

"Something's under there," he said.

"Another secret entrance," said Clarissa. "We got 'em now!"

She stepped back and examined the altar – prodded one side, kicked another impatiently. "There must be a latch or a lever."

"The cross," Wild Boy said.

"What about it?"

"Why's it so shiny? It should be covered in rust like them candlesticks. It's being used for something."

His big eyes sparkled with excitement as they roved around the gleaming bronze ornament, spotting faint finger-smudges on the shaft.

He gripped it and tried to lift it from the altar, but it seemed to be fastened to the surface. He yanked harder, and this time the cross tilted on a hinge in its base, triggering some sort of catch.

At first nothing happened. Then, gently, the altar began to tremble. Then it shook harder. Behind them, the church pews clattered together. The last shards of glass fell from the windows and shattered to the stone floor.

Wild Boy stepped back as the altar scraped to the side, revealing a dark hole in the ground.

Clarissa lowered her candle. Its light spilled down a stone ramp that led underground. "Wild Boy," she said, "that's *amazing*."

He turned and looked at her. No one had ever spoken to him like that before. Again he felt a glow of pride. But this time, he felt guilty too. Clarissa thought they were after the killer. But now, more and more, Wild Boy wanted the machine.

"Come on," he said.

They crept down the ramp until they reached a vaulted tunnel deep beneath the church. Coffins lay on stone shelves up and down the dry walls. A broken passage through some cobwebs showed where the golden-eyed man and his companions had passed. Ahead, the dim glow of their lantern lit the spider's silk an eerie orange.

Dust sprinkled from the tunnel roof as the secret entrance began to scrape shut. Wild Boy looked up the ramp, watching the rectangle of moonlight at the top get smaller as the altar slid across the gap. Then, just before it sealed, something moved through the light...

Cold fear ran down Wild Boy's spine. What had he seen? It could have been a shadow from the church, or a crow again. Or ... had someone else just come into this tunnel?

Clarissa's candle fizzled out, leaving the passage

completely dark. "Great," she said. "How are we going to catch the killer if we can't even see him? Wild Boy? Where are you?"

Reaching through the dark, Wild Boy took her hand and placed it on his arm. He didn't want to scare Clarissa by telling her what he'd seen behind them. There was enough to worry about with the golden-eyed man and his companions up ahead. But if there *was* someone else in this tunnel, they needed to get away fast.

"Come on," he said. "We gotta follow that crate."

"You mean the killer."

"Yeah, the killer."

They huddled closer and crept through the cobwebbed passage. For several minutes the only sound was their feet splashing in puddles that dotted the rough stone floor. They could still just see the golden-eyed man's light up ahead. But Wild Boy kept glancing back too. He couldn't shake the feeling that they were being followed.

The tunnel grew colder, and so narrow that they could reach out and touch both walls. Wild Boy heard a rattle of carriages, like distant thunder, on a street somewhere above. Water dripped from the ceiling, and broken chunks of stone littered the ground.

Clarissa's hand tightened on Wild Boy's arm. "I know what we should do," she whispered.

"Eh?"

"After we catch the killer, I know what we should

do. We should be partners. We could find anything, you and me. Crooks, lost dogs… People would pay us a fortune. But I'll look after the money."

Wild Boy stopped. For a second he forgot all about the men ahead, and the danger behind. "Partners?" he said.

"Yeah." Suddenly Clarissa sounded less certain. "I mean, if you wanted. But fine if you don't. I don't care neither way. In fact, forget it, will you?"

"No," Wild Boy said. "I—"

He was too stunned to speak. For so long he'd thought the only life he could ever have was alone and in a freak show. But now, maybe, there was another choice…

Just then he heard something splash in a puddle behind them. He turned and stared into the darkness. His heart began to beat harder, pounding against his ribcage.

"We gotta go faster," he breathed.

Side by side, silent, they kept going. The path began to climb again. Ahead, they saw another light in the tunnel. But it wasn't the golden-eyed man's lantern. As they crept closer, it began to take shape.

"A door," Clarissa said. "They must've gone through."

This was the end of the tunnel – an iron slab set into the rough stone wall.

Wild Boy couldn't see a handle or lock – just a tiny curling crack, no bigger than the curve of a penny, right in the centre of the door.

"There's no keyhole nowhere," Clarissa said. "I can't open it."

Wild Boy ran a finger over the crack, studying it curiously. There were tiny scratches around the edges, as if something metal had knocked against it. "I think ... I think this might be the keyhole," he said.

"Don't look like none I've ever seen."

"No. It looks like a letter..."

He brought out Doctor Griffin's ring and ran a fingertip over its raised letter *G*. Was it possible?

Clarissa turned, staring down the tunnel. "What was that?" she hissed.

"What?"

"I heard something behind us."

There it was again – footsteps splashing closer. A dark shape cut through the cobwebs.

"Wild Boy!" Clarissa said. "It's him, the hooded man!"

"Throw them rocks!"

"What?"

"Slow him down!"

Clarissa grabbed a rock from the ground and hurled it into the dark, then another and another. "He's still coming!"

Wild Boy didn't look back. He had to concentrate. He hoped he'd got this right... He slid the ring over his finger and pressed it against the crack in the door. The raised letter *G* slotted perfectly into the thin groove. "It fits!" he said.

"Open it then!"

Behind, the footsteps quickened into a run.

Wild Boy turned the ring. Immediately the iron door began to tremble. He heard the whirr of cogs turning inside, and then the *clunk, thunk* of a lock sliding.

"Got it!" he cried.

He shoved the door open and they tumbled through.

Just as they slammed it shut again, something thumped against its other side. Wild Boy and Clarissa heaved against the iron slab, struggling to keep it closed. But slowly, the door began to open.

"Push!"

"I am pushing!"

A gloved hand reached through and grasped Clarissa's hair. She screamed, and Wild Boy leaped up and bit hard into the hand's thumb. It shot back, but the door opened wider.

Wild Boy looked over his shoulder, searching for anything to use as a weapon. He saw a torch crackling on a wall. "Hold the door!" he cried.

Leaving Clarissa, he ran to the wall and snatched the torch from its bracket. Its iron handle scorched the hair on his wrist, but he held on tight as he rushed back to the door. He braced himself to stab the fire at whoever was on the other side...

But whoever it was, was gone.

Clarissa finally closed the door, and turned her pick in a lock. "It's sealed."

They leaned against it, their breaths coming in ragged gasps.

"That was him," Clarissa said. "That must have been the hooded man. But the golden-eyed man was *ahead* of us."

Wild Boy nodded, still struggling to breathe.

"That means he's not the killer. So who is?" She took the torch and raised it against the dark. "And where are we now?"

26

Wild Boy turned, taking in their new surroundings. They were in another passage, but it was very different to the rough stone tunnel they'd just passed through. The arched walls were smooth and carved at the top with faces of angels. Suits of armour stood along their sides, shimmering in the glare of fire torches that burned in iron brackets. In one direction was another metal door. In the other, a stone staircase spiralled up into the dark.

"Maybe we should get the police," Clarissa said. "Tell them that the killer's in that tunnel. They could catch him."

There was no way Wild Boy was going to the police. He didn't think they'd believe him even if he turned up with the hooded man wrapped in ribbons. "No," he said. "The golden-eyed man will help us. He was after the killer an' all. It's him we gotta find."

But that wasn't the only reason he wanted to find that man. The golden-eyed man was clearly in charge of the Gentlemen, and the Gentlemen had the machine. It was close, Wild Boy was sure.

"So which way did he go?" Clarissa said.

Wild Boy took another torch from the wall and swept the light around the ground. The Gentlemen carrying the crate had left heavy footprints in the dust near the iron door. But he couldn't see any marks from the golden-eyed man's cane.

He turned. At the bottom of the stairs, another torch was missing from its bracket. He moved towards it, his eyes raking the floor for fresh clues.

"This way," he said.

Clarissa followed him up the corkscrew passage. Their torches flickered, and shadows writhed on the walls. Distant noises drifted down the twisting staircase – the murmur of voices, and a buzzing like a swarm of bees.

And then, from behind them, a loud *clank*.

"That sounded like the tunnel door," Clarissa said.

They listened for a moment, but the only sounds were those voices, and the buzzing, and the quickening of their own breaths.

"You scared?" Clarissa whispered.

Wild Boy nodded. Blooming right he was. But he was also more determined than ever to find out what was happening here. His torch spluttered and fizzed. Raising the smoky light, he continued up the stairs – one step at a time, stopping, listening, moving on.

They came to a sliver of window, no wider than an arrow loop. Eager to get his bearings, Wild Boy peered through. What he saw made no sense. They were high up now, looking out across a patchwork of rooftops that spread towards the Thames. Below was a cobbled courtyard surrounded by high walls, round stone bastions and spiked iron gates. A clutter of buildings hugged the wall – a stone chapel, a brick bungalow and wooden stables. Ravens hopped around the cobbles, pecking for scraps.

"Looks like we're in … *a castle*," Wild Boy said.

"We can't be. There ain't no castles in London."

There was one, Wild Boy knew, but they couldn't be *there*.

The ravens flapped away as another top-hatted Gentleman wheeled a wooden cart from one of the stables, carrying something large covered in a cloth. As the cart rattled on the cobbles, the cloth slipped and Wild Boy caught a glimpse of the object beneath. It was only a brief glance but he was sure he saw a furry amber paw.

"A *tiger*?" Clarissa said.

Wild Boy remembered the remains of the experiments in Doctor Griffin's secret room – tests on human body parts and animals. "Let's keep going," he said.

The stairs ended in a vaulted corridor with rusty doors set into the walls. Wild Boy stood up on tip-toes to peer through a small barred hatch in one of the doors. The room inside was dark and dingy. There was an iron truckle-bed against a wall, a bare table and a broken bucket oozing excrement.

"Looks like a gaol cell," he said.

Clarissa elbowed him aside to see. "Another horrid room," she said. "Why do these Gentlemen always—"

A face burst into the hatch. Clarissa screamed, but before she could step back a hand shot through and grabbed her neck. A prisoner's face leered between the bars – bloodshot eyes, boils and insect bites.

"*Kill me*," he hissed.

Wild Boy dropped his torch and punched the man's hand. "Get off her!" he yelled. "Get your hands off her!"

The prisoner let go, and Wild Boy and Clarissa tumbled back against the wall.

"You all right?" Wild Boy said, helping her stand.

Clarissa nodded, but she didn't look all right. Her face had turned as white as snow as she stared at the cell door. The prisoner had slumped against the other side, and they could hear him thumping the wall, and sobbing. Wild Boy remembered Doctor Griffin's journal, and the graves at St Mary Somerset. Was this man another "subject" for the Gentlemen's machine?

"Let's get out of here," Clarissa said.

She tugged Wild Boy's arm, pulling him along the corridor. They hurried past more locked doors, heard prisoners muttering inside the cells.

Clarissa stopped. "Wrong way," she said.

The corridor ended at a stone balcony that overlooked some sort of hall. That was where the noises were coming from – the buzzing and the voices. The air here was hazy and smelled of smoke.

"How do we get out?" Clarissa said. "I don't wanna be here no more. We should get the police, tell them what's happening."

Wild Boy knew she was right. But he had to see. He had to know if it was true. *The machine what changes you…*

As he moved towards the balcony, a burst of blue light caught him in terrified silhouette.

Clarissa shielded her eyes. "What was that? Wild Boy, come back!"

Her protests were drowned by the noise from the hall, like angry insects all around them. Another flash of light shot along the corridor, but this time Wild Boy didn't flinch. He didn't even blink. He just stared into the stone hall.

Rising in front of him was the machine.

27

It looked like a metal brain.

A great knot of twisting pipes, grinding cogs and spinning dials. As big as a fairground caravan, it hung on an axle between two silver wheels. Each wheel was the size of a watermill, and held up by a towering industrial piston that rose and fell with a spit of steam and a slow *vrump, vrump, vrump*. In the middle, the metal brain trembled and buzzed.

The machine was coming to life.

Wild Boy gripped the edge of the balcony. Everything that had happened to him in the past week had been because of this machine. This was what the hooded man was trying to find. This was why the Professor and the Doctor had been killed.

As the machine's pistons pumped, its wheels turned. Crackles of blue light fizzed from the rims, shot along the axles, and disappeared inside the metal ball.

Clarissa gripped Wild Boy's arm. "What *is* that?"

"It's electricity," Wild Boy said. "It's filling with electricity."

In the hall below, men in frock coats rushed around the base of the pistons, tightening screws and reading dials. Shaded spectacles protected their eyes from the light as electrical fire shot from the giant wheels and into the tangle of pipes.

The crate that the men had carried from the church lay open and empty on the hall floor. Its cargo was strapped to a table beneath the machine.

It was the body of Doctor Griffin.

The Doctor's whiskers remained bushy and vibrant, but the face beneath them had turned grey with decay. A chunk of rotten flesh had peeled from its nose, exposing glistening white bone beneath.

Bound to the table beside the corpse was the tiger. Judging from the heavy rise and fall of its chest, the animal had been drugged.

"What are they doing?" Clarissa said. "What are they doing to that poor tiger?"

Both the tiger and the Doctor had mechanical devices fixed to their heads – steel helmets with cogs and springs around the brim, and copper rods sticking from the top. Wires rose in tight lines from the rods and up to the ball of machinery above, connecting the tiger and the corpse to the machine.

"Wild Boy," Clarissa said, tugging his sleeve. "Let's get the police."

But her words were lost to the *vrump, vrump, vrump* of the pistons. All around the machine, crackles of light gathered into angry balls of blue fire, swirling together.

The heat singed the hairs on Wild Boy's face. The noise – a buzz, then a hum and then a pulsing drone – throbbed inside his skull. Clarissa curled up beside him and covered her head. But Wild Boy forced himself to watch, even though it felt like his eyes were being stabbed with hot needles.

All around the hall, torches fell from their brackets and fizzled out. The light from the machine filled the whole space, so bright that the walls and the balcony shone brilliant blue.

Vrump, vrump, vrump…

Still the wheels turned faster.

Vrump, vrump, vrump…

Still the pipes grew brighter.

Even in shaded spectacles, the men struggled against the light. One of them shielded his face and stepped closer to the table. He reached up and gripped a lever on the tiger's helmet.

Vrump, vrump, vrump…

Another man cried, "Now!"

The rods in the helmet shot down. Over the drone of the machine, Wild Boy heard the tiger wake and roar as the metal spikes drove into its head. Streams of electrical fire shot from the ball of pipes and blasted into the poor cat's brain. The tiger shook.

More and more blue light rushed into its body until the whole animal glowed.

Clarissa shot up and screamed, "Stop! Stop it!"

There was a loud *whoomp* and the light cut out.

The pistons hissed. The wheels ground to a halt. The tiger gave a feeble whimper, and slumped back to the table.

The tiger did not move.

The machine stood still.

The hall was silent and dark.

Wild Boy heard Clarissa's breathing going even faster than his own. He touched her arm and she flinched. "What happened?" she said. "What did they just do?"

Down in the hall, a flash of orange light broke the dark as the men re-lit the torches. One of them edged closer to the tiger and placed a stethoscope cautiously to its side.

"The cat?" another of the men asked.

"Dead."

"And the Doctor?"

The man put his stethoscope to the corpse. Then he stepped back.

Wild Boy's fingers tightened around the edge of the balcony. "Did you see that?" he gasped.

"What?" Clarissa said.

Now she saw it too.

One of the Doctor's hands moved. His grey fingers strained at the straps, curling like claws.

"His eyes," Wild Boy said. "Look at his eyes!"

The Doctor's eyes had opened. Blazing with ferocity, they glared at the men around him. His lips peeled back and he bared his teeth like fangs. A growl rose from his throat – a feral, savage growl that snarled around the hall, causing the men to leap back in fright.

The Doctor slumped back to the table. His legs and arms began to shake.

"The Principal's not fixed!" one of the men cried. "Secure it! Morphine!"

The others grappled frantically with the convulsing body, but they were too late. The corpse had stopped moving. Its head lolled. Doctor Griffin was dead again.

One of the men removed his spectacles. "Bring another animal," he said. "Tell Marcus we are not ready for further human trials."

Clarissa dragged Wild Boy away from the balcony, her face as pale as the corpse. "Doctor Griffin…" she said. "That machine brought him back to life. But he sounded like … like…"

"Like the tiger," Wild Boy said.

"He *became* the tiger?"

Wild Boy gazed into the hall as a spark of electricity crackled over one of the wheels and then fizzled out. Even though he had seen it with his own eyes, he could barely believe it. The machine didn't seem to work, but it existed. And the Doctor's notes said it *had* worked, it *could* work.

He and Clarissa had hoped to save themselves by catching the killer, but Wild Boy couldn't put the clues together. Instead, wasn't this machine a better way out – a machine that changes you, transferring your mind into a different body? If he was no longer a freak, he wouldn't be hunted. He could live a normal life.

His eyes glinted in the machine's brilliant sparks. "It *is* possible," he said.

Clarissa's tongue flicked over her broken tooth. *"What* is possible?"

"The machine. I could use it on myself."

"What? Are you insane?"

The idea thrilled Wild Boy but scared him too. He closed his eyes, trying to stop his head from spinning. "The Doctor said it could work."

"But it *doesn't*!" Clarissa spat. "You saw what just happened. This is dangerous, Wild Boy! These *people* are dangerous. Catching the killer, *that's* how we're going to get out of this."

"But what if they can make the machine work? What if they could *really* make it change people?"

"We don't need it though. We can still catch the hooded man. We're partners, remember?"

Wild Boy was so confused, so tired. Clarissa kept saying they were partners, but it wasn't that simple. She was normal and he was a freak. But he could change; he could be like everyone else.

"Wild Boy," Clarissa said, "you seen what that electricity does. It goes into people's brains. What if you never think the same way again? What if you lose your skill?"

"I don't care…"

"Yes, you do!" She stepped closer and shoved him furiously in the chest. "I seen how it makes you feel. I seen it in your eyes and your smile when you're using it. It's like how I feel when I'm up on the highwire. Nothing else matters, not my mother or my father or nothing in the world. I'm proud of what I am, and you should be too. That skill is what makes you *you*."

"No!" Wild Boy said. He grabbed the thick hair on his face and pulled it angrily. "*This* is what makes me *me*."

"You don't think that," Clarissa insisted. "Not no more, not after all this."

Part of him knew she was right. But all that time he'd spent watching people, this was what he'd dreamed of – a chance to be normal.

"I gotta try, Clarissa."

Clarissa jabbed him again. Her freckles flared with anger. "Well, you use the machine then, see if it kills you. I'm gonna catch the killer myself. And when I do, I ain't gonna tell no one that you're innocent, so they'll still think you're a monster."

"Shut your head!"

"No! And even if the machine does work, it

won't save you cos you'll always be mean and a thickhead!"

Before Wild Boy could stop himself, he shoved her back. A sharp crack rang out as her head hit the wall. Clarissa slumped down and clutched the back of her skull. Blood trickled between her fingers.

Wild Boy stepped closer, shaking. What had he done? "I'm sorry," he said. "Don't you understand? I don't wanna be Wild Boy no more."

She looked up. Tears slid down her cheeks. "I *liked* Wild Boy."

He thought she was going to scream at him. He *wanted* her to scream at him. But instead she rose and staggered away down the corridor.

"Wait!" Wild Boy called. "Clarissa, it ain't safe here."

"Let her go," a voice said.

Wild Boy whirled around in fright. He recognized that cold steel voice.

The man with the golden eyeball stepped from the shadows. "You are right," he said. "It is not safe here at all."

28

"The famous Wild Boy of London. We meet again."
The man with the golden eyeball limped closer, leaning heavily on his cane. He wore the same shaded spectacles as his colleagues in the hall. The dark lenses gleamed as, beyond the balcony, another crackle of electricity lit the towering wheels of the machine.

He extended a hand. "It is a pleasure."

The fog in Wild Boy's head cleared, and his mind came into sharp focus. He considered making a run for it, but he knew the man had a sword in his cane, as well as a pistol in his coat. He wouldn't be able to escape. He had to fight. He'd go to shake his hand, but instead kick his knee and shove him back.

"No doubt," the man said, "you are considering an attack. I wonder, have you already established your method of escape? There is a secret door just yards from where you stand. Had you observed?"

"I bloomin' seen it."

"Indeed." The man stepped aside, gesturing with a sweep of his cane. "Then you are free to leave."

Wild Boy didn't move.

"It is no trick," the man said. "You have my word that you will not be harmed."

"Your word don't mean nothing to me! Who the hell are you?"

"My name is Marcus Bishop."

"Never heard of you!"

"But you have been following me."

The man struck the flint on a lantern. The light made him wince. He lowered the shutter to a dim glow and raised it against the wall. "I wonder," he said. "Have you also detected which stone triggers the door?"

Even though he had, Wild Boy stayed silent. He knew that if the man had wanted to kill him, he would have done so already. But that didn't mean he trusted him.

"I imagine that you have many questions," said the golden-eyed man. He pressed the end of his cane against one of the stones, and a slab of wall scraped away, exposing a dark passage beyond. "I will endeavour to answer as many as I can. In return, I simply ask that you walk with me."

"I ain't going nowhere with you."

"Then farewell, Wild Boy. It really was a pleasure."

The man's coat fluttered as he disappeared into the secret passage.

Wild Boy stood alone, stunned. Part of him wanted to turn and run. But still he wanted answers – about the murders and about the machine.

He crept through the narrow entrance and peered down another twisting stairway. The golden-eyed man stood a few steps below, his lantern flooding the passage with light. He knew Wild Boy would follow.

"Be careful," he said.

He set off again, his silver hair brushing the ceiling of the low passage.

Wild Boy moved faster, catching up. "Where are we?" he demanded.

"You know where we are."

"The Tower of London."

"Correct. Specifically we are in the White Tower, the castle's keep."

"You can't just do what you want in the Tower of London."

"Yes, we can."

The stairs led to a wider corridor, with swords and shields displayed on the walls. Wild Boy stopped, looked back and forth, then followed again. The golden-eyed man – *Marcus Bishop* – didn't slow down.

"Who are you?" Wild Boy said. "You and them other blokes?"

"We have no official name. Those aware of our existence simply refer to us as the Gentlemen. We work for the government."

"What government?"

"Your government."

"I ain't got no blasted government. What are you lot? Scientists, like the Professor?"

The man paused for a moment, selecting his words carefully. "Some of us. We are experts in various fields – science, medicine, military, espionage. We study new technologies, and assist the police in matters that are beyond their powers and abilities. One might describe us simply as a society of concerned individuals."

"Concerned about what?"

"Britain. Its security, prosperity, survival. You are a citizen of the largest empire the world has ever known. Such power is not acquired only by good manners."

"I seen your good manners," Wild Boy said. "I seen them prisoners you got locked up. You're gonna use the machine on them once you got it working."

"Our subjects are all convicted criminals, sentenced to death by the courts. Each has been offered a choice. Should the machine prove successful in transferring them into a new body, they will be granted a stay of execution. If not, a Christian burial. Are those not more generous terms than the hangman offers?"

They came to a door. Marcus Bishop tapped his cane against the iron surface.

"What's any of this got to do with me?" Wild Boy said.

"Nothing whatsoever. You are the one who involved yourself the moment you stole that letter from Charles Griffin. And I am afraid you are now involved rather deeply indeed."

The door swung open. Wild Boy followed the man into the vast cavity of the tower's stone hall.

"I heard what you said to Miss Everett," Marcus said. "You wish to use the machine upon yourself. That could indeed be an effective way of escaping your predicament. But Miss Everett is correct too. The machine is as likely to destroy you as it is to save you. Almost certainly your mind will never function in the same way again."

Wild Boy looked up at the colossal wheels of the Gentlemen's machine. Clarissa's words kept ringing in his head, but he tried to forget them and remember how badly he wanted to be normal.

The pistons slowly began to pump again, the wheels turned and steam hissed from the ball of twisting pipes. "How does it work?" he asked.

Marcus Bishop smiled. "First, permit me to ask a question of my own." A blue spark crackled around the pipes, reflecting off his dark lenses. "What do you know of electricity?"

29

Clarissa Everett had never been so angry in her life.

Wild Boy was a liar and a thug. They were meant to be finding the killer, but all he cared about was that stupid machine. What an idiot he was to think he could change. He'd always be a thickhead!

A rush of wind sent an eerie howl along the corridor. Clarissa's head pounded with pain. She wiped a trickle of blood from above her eyes. She was furious with him, but she wished he was here now. She'd stormed off in such a hurry – running past those prisoners, down one passage and another – she'd not paid any attention to where she was going. How could she get out of here without him?

Maybe there was another secret door, she thought. These Gentlemen were obsessed with them. How did Wild Boy find them? She ran a hand along the wall, prodding stones, kicking others, kicking harder in frustration.

No – she had to calm down and think. That's what he always did.

Think!

A window!

If she could find a window, she could climb out. She was an acrobat after all – heights didn't trouble her. She could scale any surface, balance on ledges and jump at least thirty feet without injury, just like her father and her mother. *He* couldn't do that!

Another few steps and she came to a door. She felt a breeze coming from underneath. There had to be a window on the other side. She was proud of that bit of thinking – better than any *he'd* have done in the circumstances. He'd have started swearing and getting angry.

She took out her picks and unlocked the door.

He couldn't do *that* either.

The door creaked open. Murky morning light cast a window-shadow on a long mahogany table. Antique rifles and pistols hung in rows on the walls. At the other end of the table, another door was open a fraction. Clarissa considered it, but decided that the window was still her best chance of escape.

The window opened easily, and misty drizzle speckled her face. Outside, the sky was as grey as the walls that surrounded the courtyard. She could just see a stagnant pond following the curve of the wall to the other side. It looked like a moat. But this *couldn't* be a castle, could it?

More than ever she wanted to get out of here.

The stones would be slippery but she was confident she could climb down, jump to the wall and into the moat on the other side. She turned to slide out.

And her grip tightened on the window frame.

At the other end of the room, the door slowly opened. A cloaked figure stepped from beyond.

In a rush of panic, Clarissa tried to climb from the window. But she was shaking with fear. Her grip slipped and she tumbled onto the floor beside the table. She scrambled back and bashed against the wall. She was too scared to get up, too terrified even to scream.

The hooded man towered over her.

A breeze rustled from the window, blowing the killer's long leather shroud. The cloak flapped open – just for a second, but for long enough...

Clarissa stared, barely able to believe what she had seen beneath that cloak. *Who* she had seen. "No," she breathed. "It's *you*."

30

A flash of electricity lit one of the pipes on the Gentlemen's machine. Marcus Bishop removed his spectacles, and the brilliant blue light glinted off his golden eyeball.

"What do you know of electricity?" he asked again.

Even through his thick hair Wild Boy felt a blast of heat. The machine towered in front of him like some giant industrial engine, almost filling the hall. Several Gentlemen rushed about its base – reading dials, inspecting fittings and adjusting fixtures on the mechanical helmets that had been strapped to the tiger and Doctor Griffin's corpse.

"Perhaps you observed some of Henry's performances at the fair?" Marcus asked.

"You mean Professor Wollstonecraft?"

"Indeed. Henry pioneered our understanding of electricity."

Electricity, Wild Boy thought. That strange new force was at the heart of all of this. "Don't know nothing about it," he said. "Some clever new science."

"Not new. Electricity is older than mankind. Indeed, electricity *is* mankind. Allow me to ask you another question. Why do *you* wish to use the machine?"

Wild Boy looked up sharply. He saw himself reflected in Marcus's golden eye – a mess of hair and dirt, in his tatty red and gold coat. "Cos I'm a freak," he said. "Cos I'm being hunted by half the city. Cos some mad killer set me up just cos I look different to other people."

"Is that all you see yourself as?" Marcus said. "A freak? No, I agree with Miss Everett. I do not think that is how you feel. It is, perhaps, how you felt once."

Wild Boy remembered Clarissa's words before she left him. "So?" he said.

"So, you have survived for days with half of London on your scent. Not only survived, but pieced together the clues that led you here, solved the mystery of your predicament and asked several questions to which I believe you already knew the answer."

"What of it?"

"Do you not grasp my point? A human body is flesh and bones. But a *human being* is his thoughts, memories, reason and beliefs. All of these things, however, are simply electrical pulses shooting around the brain."

Marcus stepped to a table that was cluttered with parts from the machine. He picked up a copper rod, and touched it against a thick coil of silver wire. A blue spark zapped from the end.

"Who you are and how you think is all electricity," he said. "Fireworks in your brain. We call it the Life Principal. You might call it the mind. Others of a more spiritual disposition call it the soul."

The soul. Wild Boy shuddered. "This thing sucks it out, don't it?"

"Crudely put, but accurate. The wheels act as dynamos, channelling electricity into precise points in a subject's cranium. It fuses with the human electricity inside the brain. Both are extracted, and then transferred into the receiver's body."

Marcus zapped the metal rod again. "Thus the whole individual is relocated to a new body – his thoughts, memories, reason and beliefs."

It changes you, Wild Boy thought. He could still hardly believe it was possible. "But why? Why build it?"

"I will not pretend that such a device does not have certain military applications," Marcus replied, "but can you not imagine the good it could also achieve? The sick taken from failing bodies. Cripples made to walk." He tapped the rod against his false eyeball. "The blind to see."

"Did Professor Wollstonecraft build it?"

"It was his design," Marcus said. "But he was unhappy with it. He made plans to rebuild the machine, a much smaller device but even more powerful. However, Charles – Doctor Griffin – would not allow it. So Henry left our organization, taking his plans with him."

"He joined the circus," Wild Boy said.

The golden-eyed man smiled. "He always was an old romantic. Sadly he was also a hopeless drunk with an utter disregard for our oath of secrecy. It seems he spoke about the machine to the wrong person."

"The hooded man," Wild Boy said.

Marcus nodded. "Shortly after Henry left us, he was proved correct. There was an overload in one of the machine's capacitors, and it has not functioned correctly since. We believe that the killer is using the Professor's plans to build a machine that works. But he cannot do so without the crowns."

"Crowns?"

Marcus raised the rod and prodded one of the mechanical helmets that hung on wires from the machine. "*Crowns*," he said. "They are not in the Professor's plans."

A valve on the machine burst, blasting an angry jet of steam. The other Gentlemen rushed about as they struggled to contain the malfunction. Only Wild Boy and Marcus remained calm, watching the commotion from the side of the hall.

"I can tell you this," said Marcus. "I have no intention whatsoever of letting you use the machine. And I do not believe that you truly wish to use it either."

He was right. Wild Boy had known since the moment he pushed Clarissa against the wall. The look in her eyes… It was as if it had woken him from a daze. They were partners, and they had got close to unmasking the killer. Maybe they could have done it too, but he had let her down.

Marcus placed the rod back on the table. "May I ask what clues you and Miss Everett have discovered so far regarding this hooded man?"

Instinct urged Wild Boy not to tell the man anything. But he was so tired. He felt as if the clues were slipping away. He needed help. "There's one thing I can't make sense of," he said. "The killer disappeared in an alley, just vanished, and he dropped the Doctor's notebook."

"Dropped it?"

"I thought it was because he'd already read it. Only, he couldn't have. We were chasing him."

Another smile flashed across Marcus's tight face. "And this book led you here?" he asked.

"What's so funny?" Wild Boy demanded.

"You see so much, Wild Boy, yet I fear you have been blind to the utterly obvious. Do you really believe the killer dropped that book?"

"I dunno…"

"Yes, you do."

Right then, a realization shot through Wild Boy, as bright as a spark from the machine. He saw now what he'd been too lost in self-pity to notice before: not only why the killer had dropped the book, but also why his own name had been written at the crime scenes...

"Of course," he said. "Of course!"

He had been used. He'd been lured to the Doctor's house to find the secret room. Then the killer had *deliberately* left the book in that alley, drawing his attention to the name of St Mary Somerset church. And there, Wild Boy had found the entrance to the tunnel...

He hadn't been set up because he was a *freak*, he realized. He'd been set up because he was *unique*, the only person who could read the clues. He'd led the hooded man straight to this machine.

Wild Boy turned, his eyes wide with panic. "He's here," he said. "He's in the tunnel."

Marcus simply tilted his head, as if to suggest the matter was dealt with. He raised a hand and showed Wild Boy the ring on his finger, the raised letter *G*. "As you know, this is a very difficult place to enter without the correct key. We are safe for now. I have sent men to—"

"No," Wild Boy said. "He stole the Professor's ring. He has the correct key. He's *already* here."

"Indeed I am," said a voice.

The hooded man appeared on the balcony.

Clarissa stood beside him, bound by a rope that pinned her arms to her sides. A rag around her mouth smothered her cries.

Beneath the killer's hood, the white mask peered down into the hall – first at Wild Boy, then at Marcus Bishop and finally at the machine. His muffled voice echoed around the stone walls. "At last."

The Gentlemen reached into their coats for their weapons. But the hooded man raised a knife to Clarissa's neck, and they hesitated.

"I have not harmed her," the killer said. "If you wish it to remain that way, I suggest you do exactly as I say. Especially you, Wild Boy."

Wild Boy was desperate to make a run for the stairs, to save Clarissa. But he couldn't risk the killer using that blade. He had to think, find a way to save her.

"What?" he said. "What do you want?"

"You have proved extremely helpful to me so far," the hooded man replied, "by finding the clues that led me here. Now I must ask one final favour."

With his free hand, he threw a sack over the balcony. It landed on the floor by Wild Boy's feet. "Remove the crowns from the machine and put them in that bag."

"You swear you'll let her go?" Wild Boy said.

"You have my word," the hooded man replied.

Marcus Bishop stepped forward. "Do not do it," he warned.

But there was no choice. Wild Boy didn't care about the machine any more – the killer could have every piece of it as long as he set Clarissa free. He grabbed the sack and ran to the mechanical helmets that hung from the machine's pipes. He had no idea how to detach them, and no time to work it out. So he simply jumped up and tore the devices from their wires.

"Wild Boy," Marcus insisted. "He will not release Miss Everett."

Wild Boy barely heard him. He stuffed the crowns in the sack and rushed back across the hall. By the time he returned, a rope hung from the balcony.

"Tie the sack on," the hooded man instructed.

Wild Boy did. As it rose, he looked up at Clarissa. She was staring at him, flashing urgent signals with her eyes and screaming into her gag. She was trying to tell him something, but he couldn't understand.

The sack slid over the balcony.

"Now let her go!" Wild Boy demanded.

But the killer didn't lower the knife. "Thank you," he said. "But I am afraid you should have listened to Mr Bishop. He was right, I have built a machine of my own. One that works. And now that I have the crowns, it is complete. But I need a subject for its trial run, and I believe Miss Everett would make a perfect candidate."

Wild Boy didn't look at the hooded man. He kept his eyes fixed on Clarissa. He saw tears slide down her cheeks and soak into the rag in her mouth.

"I won't let that happen," he told her. "I'll save you, I swear."

She looked at him, and he saw in her eyes that she believed him. But the hooded man dragged her back into the darkness.

"I am afraid, Wild Boy, that it *is* happening," the killer said.

"This is ridiculous," Marcus shouted. "How on earth do you expect to escape?"

The hooded man's voice came back, fainter now, moving away. "Watch and see, Mr Bishop. Watch and see."

Marcus drew a pistol from inside his jacket. He loaded the gun's plate and issued orders to the other Gentlemen to seal doors and guard exits. But as he spoke, another sound rang around the hall.

A loud, blood-curdling shriek, like a pig being slaughtered. Somewhere, a door slammed. Then another, and another, as the screeching grew louder. Wild Boy turned, listening, confused. He could hear now that the noise was a laugh. No – it was several laughs, coming closer.

"No," he gasped. "He can't have…"

"What the devil is that?" Marcus asked.

"The prisoners!" Wild Boy cried. "He's released the prisoners!"

31

Black clouds swirled over the White Tower.

The stone keep rose from the centre of the courtyard, its pinnacled turrets snarling up against the rain. Ravens hopped about the walls, untroubled by the rumbling thunder as they pecked the cobbles for scraps.

All at once, the birds flapped into the air.

A door burst open.

Marcus Bishop limped down the Tower's wooden steps and into the courtyard, barking orders to the men who followed. "Load your weapons, Gentlemen, they could already be outside. Mr Beauchamp, seal the west gate. Mr Rawlins, guard the river dock, make sure the boat is secure. Not one prisoner escapes."

Wild Boy raced behind them. "Clarissa!" he yelled. "Clarissa!"

He pushed one of the Gentlemen out of the way,

but the man shoved him back, sending him tumbling onto the stone ground. The other Gentlemen didn't have time to search for his friend. They had troubles of their own.

One of the escaped prisoners burst from the side of the tower. Chains rattled around the man's shackled wrists as he fled for the perimeter wall.

"Mr Cullen!" Marcus called.

The prisoner froze. Wild Boy saw that it was the man who had grabbed Clarissa through the hatch of his cell. The fugitive held his hands open in surrender, smiling to reveal a set of black and brown teeth. "Can't blame me for trying," he said.

Marcus nodded. Then he shot the man in the head.

The prisoner crumpled in a crimson mist.

"Gentlemen," Marcus said. "Here they come."

The keep's door flew open. Prisoners charged down the steps and into the rain. The Gentlemen ran after them, firing rifles and pistols. Another prisoner collapsed in a spray of blood. Ravens squawked in the air.

Another prisoner fell, then another. The others ran like fury around the side of the Tower, committed now to their flight – escape or die.

"Forget them!" Wild Boy screamed. "Look for Clarissa!"

But they weren't listening, and didn't care. He had to find her himself. He tried to ignore the mayhem around him, to focus his mind on the killer. He didn't think the hooded man was free yet. He would need another distraction, something even bigger than this to escape the castle walls. In a flash of horror, Wild Boy realized that there was only one thing big enough to do that.

He turned and charged back towards the White Tower. "He's inside!" he cried. "The killer's still inside!"

Only Marcus heard. Reloading his pistol, he limped after Wild Boy towards the keep. "That makes no sense," he said. "He knows our machine doesn't work. Why would he have gone back?"

Wild Boy's reply was drowned out by a loud groan that came from inside the tower, a sound like twisting metal. Around the courtyard, the Gentlemen turned. Even the fleeing prisoners looked back as the noise grew louder, echoing off the Tower's walls.

"We're too late!" Wild Boy said.

And then –

BOOM!

A sound like cannon-fire shook the courtyard. The cobbles rattled. Several of the Gentlemen fell to their backsides.

BOOM! BOOM!

It was coming from inside the White Tower. A burst of blue fire lit the ancient fortress from inside, so powerful it shattered the narrow windows. Blocks of stone crumbled from the walls and crashed to the ground.

BOOM! BOOM! BOOM!

Wild Boy stumbled and fell as the impacts sent a tremor along the ground. He rolled away as another huge stone smashed down yards from his head.

"He's using the machine!" he said.

"Let him," Marcus replied. "It will kill him."

"No! He's using it to *escape*!"

Now Marcus understood, because now it happened: an explosion of stone and steam and brilliant blue light. The side of the White Tower caved in as giant sections of machinery exploded through, flying in every direction. Pipes slammed into walls, cogs crashed into stables and a steaming piston collided with the tower's chapel, shattering its stained-glass window. Gentlemen dived aside as one of the machine's massive wheels rolled wildly across the courtyard, spitting and sparking. It careened over and slammed against the perimeter wall in a cloud of dust and steam.

Wild Boy scrambled up, struggling to see through the haze. "There!" he yelled.

The hooded man was escaping over the rubble. The killer moved awkwardly, with those heavy, limping strides. Clarissa hung over his shoulder, her fiery hair draped down the back of his cloak.

"Clarissa!" Wild Boy cried.

He raced after them, leaping piles of broken

stone. Around the courtyard, the sparks had set fire to the stables. Over the roar of the flames, Wild Boy heard gunshots coming from the Tower's dock.

"Stop him!" someone shouted. "Don't let him get away!"

But they were too late. As Wild Boy ran closer, a belch of steam rose into the rain, and a steamboat chugged out onto the Thames. The hooded man stood at the controls. Behind him, Clarissa lay on the deck. She looked up, dazed and bleary-eyed, blood dribbling from the wound on her head. For a second, she and Wild Boy locked eyes. And then she was gone as the boat disappeared into the drizzle.

Another block fell from the Tower and smashed into a pile of crates beside the dock. But Wild Boy just stood still, staring at the river. There was an empty feeling of dread in his belly, like hunger gnawing at his guts.

"Clarissa," he said.

A sheet of paper swept over the broken crates. It was her list. Wild Boy picked it up and stared at the messy writing. The clues she'd written seemed to swirl on the page. He couldn't focus, couldn't think of anything but the look on her face when he'd hurt her.

Marcus came up beside him, grimacing from the pain in his knee. He plucked the golden eyeball from its socket, dripped its liquid contents onto his coat sleeve, and inhaled deeply.

"Who is he?" he said. "Who is the hooded man?"

"I don't know," Wild Boy said. "I can't think…"

"Now is the time *to* think. Your friend's life is at stake."

Wild Boy whirled at him, crumpling the page. "You think I don't know that?" he yelled. "These clues don't make sense! How could the killer have survived that jump? How could he vanish in an alley with only rats and … and bloomin' boxes!"

He turned to kick one of the crates, but stopped. He stood still, staring at the broken boxes.

"The crates," he whispered.

At that moment, a great weight seemed to lift from his shoulders and float away. Suddenly it all made sense, and Wild Boy knew *everything*. He knew the location of the killer's machine, he knew how to save Clarissa, and – at last – he knew the identity of the hooded man. He knew it, but he could barely believe it.

He looked at Marcus as storm clouds swirled overhead. "The fair," he said. "You and me gotta go to the fair."

PART III

The

MACHINE
WHAT CHANGES
You

32

Wild Boy closed his eyes.

He breathed in deeply, scrunched them tighter. But still he saw Clarissa staring at him from that balcony, her eyes glaring and accusing. *We were partners,* they seemed to say. *We could have caught the killer. But you betrayed me, and now look what's happened.*

The hooded man had stolen the Tower's steamboat, and it had taken vital minutes for the Gentlemen to requisition another from a passing waterman. Marcus Bishop had selected his five best men and they'd set off in pursuit. Wild Boy feared they were already too late.

Rain lashed against him as he stood at the front of the boat. It was the middle of the morning but the sky was as dark as night. Gaslights blinked on the riverbanks, and thunder rumbled overhead.

He wiped wet hair from his eyes and scanned the river for the Tower's vessel. There were dozens of ships on the water – steam ferries, coal barges and trading clippers moored side by side, their tall masts creaking and swaying. Moving between them all was frustratingly slow. Wild Boy wanted to yell at the Gentlemen, but he knew they were doing everything they could. Three of the men shovelled coal into the furnace, and brown smoke belched from the steamboat's funnel.

Marcus came up beside Wild Boy. His golden eyeball glinted in the boat's lantern. "This would be easier if you told me who we are after," he said.

Who we are after. At least Wild Boy knew *that* now. But he couldn't tell Marcus the killer's identity. He didn't know for sure if he could trust him. Was the Gentleman's main concern saving Clarissa, or finding the killer's machine?

"I've just realized that I never asked your name," Marcus said.

"It's Wild Boy."

"No, I mean your real name."

His real name. He remembered all the times he'd dreamed of being someone else. But not any more. He knew now that he wasn't just a freak. He was different, and for the first time ever he was glad to be.

"My name's Wild Boy," he said firmly.

Marcus smiled. "Well then, Wild Boy, we have a

killer to catch, a friend to save and your names to clear. Are you ready for it?"

He was ready, all right. In the hectic few minutes after the hooded man escaped, Wild Boy hadn't only solved the mystery of the killer's identity; he'd also devised a plan to save Clarissa. It was risky, dangerous. But his friend was relying on him.

The boat's funnel lowered as it slipped under the sleek stone arches of London Bridge. Through the rain, he saw St Paul's Cathedral squatting like a monster over a sprawl of lanes and alleys that ran from the river. Beyond, a bright orange light flared into the sky, as if a huge bonfire was raging in the heart of the City.

"Bartholomew Fair," Wild Boy said. "That's where the killer's gone."

It hadn't been hard to work *that* out. The hooded man knew him, or at least knew of his abilities. The killer had known Professor Wollstonecraft too, so he must have lived with them at the fair. That also explained one of the clues on Clarissa's list.

Marks on killer's hood – lives in place with low ceiling.

The hooded man lived in a caravan.

They drew closer to the riverbank, and a jetty crammed with steamboats taking people to the fair. Fights had broken out among the captains jostling for space.

"Sir," one of the Gentlemen called. "Look!"

Docked among the boats was the Tower's

steamship. A golden letter *G* shone on the vessel's side – but the boat was empty.

"The dock's too busy, sir," one of the Gentlemen said. "We can't get close."

Frustration boiled inside Wild Boy. He turned to kick one of the wooden seats, but stopped himself. Getting angry wouldn't help Clarissa. He needed to think.

He turned and rushed to the side of the boat. Upstream, a rickety tavern leaned over the river, propped up by beams that jutted from the bank. The mouth of a large sewer stuck out beneath, trickling brown slush into the swirling water.

"Steer over there!" Wild Boy said. "We can get to the fair underground."

The Gentleman hesitated, reluctant to take orders from a boy. He looked to Marcus, who gave a slight, almost imperceptible, nod of his head. "Do what he says," he ordered.

With a belch of smoke, the boat turned. The paddlewheel churned through the murky water as they drew nearer to the bank. The men manoeuvred the vessel so its bow poked beneath the tavern's overhang, kissing the mouth of the sewer.

Wild Boy leaped into the tunnel from the boat, and signalled for the others to follow. "Hurry!"

One by one they came across. Crouching low, they followed Wild Boy into the reeking dark. Marcus limped behind him, one hand on his cane, the other pressed against the tunnel wall. "You know this fair well?" he asked.

Bartholomew Fair. Wild Boy knew it well enough. Through a grille he saw the dense mass of people cramming the street above. It was like a glimpse into hell – everyone pushing and barging, screeching and swearing. A man spat blood into the gutter. Medicine men sold potions from trays. A fire-eater belched flames into the driving rain.

Around a dozen travelling fairs came together for this last and largest show of the season. Shops, stalls and stages filled every available space from the river to West Smithfield, the square where Wild Boy's fair usually pitched. That, he knew, was where he needed to reach. That was where he'd save Clarissa.

Ahead, a slant of grey light broke the dark. An island of bricks rose from the sewage where part of the tunnel wall had collapsed.

"We can get up through here," he said. "We should come out close."

He crawled through the hole and into a dingy chamber. It was some sort of cellar, with rotten walls and crumbling stone stairs. It reminded Wild Boy of the place where he'd hidden with Clarissa and Sir Oswald. That seemed like a long time ago now.

Strengthened by the memory, he climbed the stairs to an abandoned shop – a shell of smashed glass, cracked mirrors and broken brick. Light shone in thin streams between the wooden planks of the boarded-up entrance.

Outside, the rain was coming down hard, but most people were too drunk to care, dancing arm-in-arm through the downpour. Over their heads Wild Boy saw the peak of Mary Everett's circus tent. That was where he needed to be, but it was a hundred yards away across the square. There was no way he'd get through these crowds, not with the reward on his head.

Marcus emerged from the stairway. Wild Boy saw the man's fingers tighten around the top of his cane, and knew the pain in his knee had grown worse.

"We're too far out," Wild Boy said. "We'll have to go back down, find another way."

"What is that over there?" Marcus said, peering between the boards.

Halfway across the square, a line of policemen struggled to clear a path for a marching band and a golden stagecoach that rode slowly through the crowd.

"That's the Mayor's carriage," Wild Boy said. He remembered how each year the Lord Mayor paraded to the circus tent to officially open the fair.

"If we can reach those police officers," Marcus said, "they will escort us to the circus tent."

"Coppers?" Wild Boy said, horrified. The only place they'd escort him to was prison.

"Believe me," Marcus explained, "the police will

do exactly as I tell them. We are a *very* powerful organization."

Wild Boy was beginning to believe that. He was keen to learn more about these Gentlemen, who could order the police about, take over the Tower of London and fill its cells with condemned criminals. But he could think about that later.

Marcus turned to the other Gentlemen as they came up the stairs. Even though their trousers dripped with filth from the sewers, the five men still looked sharp and focused.

"Gentlemen," Marcus said, "you must go ahead to the circus tent. I shall follow with Wild Boy. Have everything ready. We stick to his plan."

"Find Sir Oswald Farley," Wild Boy added. "He'll help you."

The Gentlemen hesitated, still flustered that Wild Boy was in charge. But a glare from Marcus stirred them into action. Four of them brought out their pistols and loaded the plates with powder. The other yanked away some of the panels from the shop entrance. And then they set off, pushing through the mass of bodies towards the big top.

Wild Boy's plan was underway. But it relied on him and Marcus reaching the circus too. "So how we gonna get to them coppers?" he said. "Fight our way through?"

"Fighting, Wild Boy, is not always the solution. I should think you know that by now."

Marcus gripped his cane and drew the thin steel sword from inside. "We are simply going to give them a scare," he said.

"Well, I know these types, and there ain't much what scares them."

Marcus looked at him, and another hint of a smile danced across his face. "There is *one* thing," he said.

33

"Ladies and gentlemen, please stay calm and stand away."

Startled faces stared. Frightened bodies stepped back. Someone screamed. Someone laughed. The whole crowd watched as Marcus Bishop emerged from the shop, one arm wrapped around Wild Boy's neck and gripping a pistol. The Gentleman's other hand swept his sword in a wide arc, clearing a path to move forward.

"I have captured the Wild Boy of London," he declared. "And I claim the reward. I intend to deliver him to the officers in the parade. Anyone who tries to stop me will receive a bullet in the neck. Now, please, let me pass."

Some of the crowd scoffed, thinking it a prank. This ragged, filthy boy *was* covered in hair, but surely someone so short and slim couldn't be the Wild Boy of

London, monster and murderer of two men. Marcus's sword, though, was no joke. As one, the crowd edged back farther, making way for the Gentleman.

"Back!" Marcus said. "You, fat lady, stand aside!"

The fat lady stood aside. Everyone stood aside, parting like the Red Sea to let them through. As the crowd pressed back, the chain of policemen struggled to keep them from spilling into the route of the Lord Mayor's coach parade.

Wild Boy struggled to breathe in Marcus's powerful grip. He was amazed by how well this was working. It wasn't just the weapons that held the mob back. It was Marcus – the force of his words. He'd never seen someone in such complete command.

But he knew it wouldn't last. The reward on his head was too high.

Some of the crowd edged closer. Clammy hands reached for him. Hot faces leered. Marcus cracked one man on the head with his pistol, but still they came.

"Get the freak!" someone yelled. "Split the reward!"

Wild Boy kicked another man, who lunged at him. But there were too many. They grabbed his arms, dragging him from Marcus's grip.

"Shoot!" Wild Boy yelled.

"What?" Marcus said.

"Shoot your bloomin' gun!"

It was their last chance. Raising his pistol, Marcus fired into the sky.

The crowd reeled back, tumbling into one another.

The police couldn't hold them any longer. The blue line broke and bodies sprawled past. They collided with the marching band, sending tubas and trombones clattering.

"Now!" Wild Boy cried.

Bursting forward, he ran over the backs of the crowd and into the path of the parade. He pelted towards the circus tent, between the two lines of police. The officers saw him but they couldn't break their chain without letting the rest of the crowd swamp the procession.

"It's the Wild Boy of London!" someone shouted.

"He's after the Mayor!"

But the Mayor was far behind. Wild Boy's lungs burned and his legs strained. As he got near the big top, he saw a familiar figure waiting at the entrance. Sir Oswald hopped on one hand, and waved urgently with the other.

"Master Wild!" he said. "Thank the heavens you are safe. But where is Miss Everett? And what is this business? These gentlemen ordered me to bring Mr Finch to the circus. They said it was upon your request. Surely he is the last person you would wish to see right now."

Wild Boy leaned against the circus pay box, catching his breath. Now that he was here, he was more scared than ever about what he had to do. He looked at Sir Oswald, wondering if he should tell him what he knew about the killer. But he decided to stick to his plan. "I don't have much time," he gasped. "I'll explain inside."

Even in the spluttering light of the gas chandelier, the circus tent was dark and dank. Rainwater leaked through holes high in the canvas, turning the sawdust into slush. The other Gentlemen were here, guarding two prisoners in the middle of the ring – Augustus Finch and Mary Everett.

The showman and ringmaster looked almost amused by the Gentlemen's pistols. Both of them were well used to run-ins with the law. But when they saw Wild Boy, their faces changed. Mary Everett's mouth curled from a sneer into something like a snarl, the crust of powder make-up cracking across her cheeks. Finch glared at Wild Boy, stroking the deep purple scar that ran over his nose. His other hand slid towards his waistcoat, inside which Wild Boy knew the showman kept his favourite knife.

Marcus came up behind Wild Boy, breathing hard. He gripped one of the chandelier's guy ropes, and winced from the pain in his knee. "Are you sure you know what you are doing?" he said.

Wild Boy nodded, although suddenly he wasn't sure at all. Ever since the Tower he'd been running on anger and adrenalin, barely stopping to think. Now he felt sick with fear – of the mob behind him and of the killer, who was just yards away from him now, in this tent.

"Well then," Marcus said. "This is your show, Wild Boy. Shall we begin?"

34

Augustus Finch and Mary Everett.

Seeing them together, Wild Boy didn't know who presented the more grotesque figure – Finch, with his black and white hair and his scars all shiny across his face, or Mary Everett, who watched him from behind her thick white make-up. They would have made a fine couple. Both, he thought, were quite capable of murder.

Mary Everett lit a cigar and blew smoke into the face of her Gentleman guard. If she was worried by the man's pistol, she didn't show it. "So, freak," she growled at Wild Boy, "you're in charge now, are you? You gonna tell us what this is about?"

Wild Boy stepped closer, trying not to show his fear. He looked the ringmaster straight in the eye. "You know what this is about," he said. "Murder."

"Ha! You ain't pinning no murder on me."

"You pinned one on *me*," Wild Boy said.

"That was Showman's Law. It was right and proper."

Showman's Law, Wild Boy thought. It was her twisted idea of justice that had let the killer escape undetected. Until now.

He brought out the list of clues.

The page trembled in his hands as he read it again, silently to himself, making absolutely certain that he'd got this right.

Clues so far

- Killer walks funny
- Killer knew the Professor
- Marks in mud by Professor's body - from a cane?
- Marks on killer's hood - lives in place with low ceiling
- Hair by Doctor's body - silver or white?
- Killer can jump like me
- He can disappear! Or it might be a trick

"Master Wild?" Sir Oswald asked. Wild Boy's friend sat on the stumps of his thighs at the side of the ring, watching with worried eyes. "What is that paper?"

"This is Clarissa's list," Wild Boy said.

"Clarissa?" said Mary Everett.

"Your daughter. The one you set the dogs after, remember?"

"She sided with a freak."

"No. She sided with a friend."

The ringmaster snorted. "So you really think it was me that done them killings?"

Marcus limped forward on his cane. "You are a suspect. After all, you knew about Wild Boy's abilities."

"When I was in that cage," Wild Boy explained, "you said to me, *I'm told you can see things no one else can.*"

"Ha! That all the evidence you got?" Mary Everett asked.

"No, I got plenty more. See them marks in the sawdust? If you didn't know they was from your crutch, you might think they looked like marks from a cane. And you were an acrobat once, weren't you? You're trained to make high jumps, just like the one the killer made from the Doctor's house."

Wild Boy stepped so close that her cigar smoke tickled the hairs on his face. "Why do you hide your face?" he said.

"Say that again, freak?"

"Ever since Clarissa's father left, you've hidden your face behind that powder. Is it because you blame yourself, or you hate yourself? Maybe you wish you were someone else, the sort of person your husband *wouldn't* have run away from. Maybe you used to drink with Professor Wollstonecraft. And maybe you discovered his plans to build a new machine…"

Mary Everett looked to the ground. Flakes of make-up fell from her face. When she spoke again her voice had lost its venom. It was soft, distant. "I… I don't know what you're talking about."

Wild Boy wondered if buried somewhere beneath that make-up was the mother Clarissa once loved. "What happened to you?" he said. "Why do you hate Clarissa so much?"

The ringmaster looked up, and now her eyes burned like hot coals. "She sided against me," she said. "She sided with *him*. She sided with her father. You see her again, freak, you tell her that. You tell her I ain't her mother no more."

She flicked her cigar at him, and the ash burned the hairs on his face. Wild Boy staggered back, but resisted the urge to fight. He had to stay focused on the killer.

Marcus placed a hand on his shoulder. "What about Finch?"

This whole time, Augustus Finch hadn't said a word. He'd just stared at Wild Boy, still running a finger over his longest scar. But now, finally, he spoke.

"Yeah. What about me?"

"There's evidence against you an' all," Wild Boy said, holding the showman's glare. "That hair at the Doctor's house – maybe it was white. The killer has a funny walk and you been limping ever since I cut your foot. And you got hobnails on your boots – they could look like cane marks on the ground. And you would have known about my skill – maybe from when you heard me and Sir Oswald talking. Maybe you're the murderer."

One of the Gentlemen raised his pistol, warning the showman to stay put. But Wild Boy knew that even a gun wouldn't stop Augustus Finch when his blood was up. So what happened next came as little surprise.

Finch pulled the knife from inside his waistcoat. "I'll show you murder, you ugly mutt!" he spat. He rushed forward and lunged at Wild Boy.

But before the showman had taken three steps, Marcus lashed out with his sword. The Gentleman was so fast that even Wild Boy's quick eyes saw only a blur of metal and a spurt of blood.

Finch fell back with a cry, the sawdust speckled crimson. A new cut had opened across his cheek – a bloody, dripping letter G.

Sir Oswald rushed forward on his hands and snatched away the showman's knife. "Master Wild? Are you hurt?"

Wild Boy looked at Sir Oswald, and slowly shook his head.

Marcus wiped his sword with his handkerchief. "You were right," he said to Wild Boy. "He did attack."

He stood over the wounded showman and slid his sword back into its cane. "Augustus Tiberius Finch," Marcus said. "You were named after Roman emperors. Your father must have had high expectations of you. Alas, he could not see past the birthmark that covered your cheek. Ever since, you have tried to hide it, picking fights to add new scars to your face. One might say that you have scratched away your past. I wonder, do you dream of being the sort of man of whom your father would have approved? Do you, too, dream of being someone else? Is that why *you* wanted the machine?"

Wild Boy expected the showman to fight back. But instead Finch curled up tighter in the sawdust, hiding his face with his bloodied hands.

"No…" he whimpered.

And then he started to cry.

Despite everything, Wild Boy felt sorry for him. Finch's life, too, had been defined by the way he looked. Until now, Wild Boy had never realized what a tragic man it had made him.

But there was someone else Wild Boy needed to speak to. "And what about you," he said, "Marcus Bishop?"

Marcus's single eye turned to him curiously. "Me again?"

"There's as much evidence against you as anyone else. The cane marks, the hair, the way the killer limped. And that jump from the Doctor's window… That's possible if you're drugged up on laudanum and don't feel pain."

"Except of course that I was beside you when the killer took Miss Everett."

"So maybe you were in it with another of these Gentlemen," Wild Boy said. "Maybe you set it all up, created a killer so you could steal the machine's crowns without anyone else knowing."

"And my motive?"

"Your eye and your knee. I seen how much pain they give you. Maybe you wanted a new body. Or maybe it's about money. You were gonna sell the new machine for the highest offer."

"A traitor?" Marcus said. "Now that *is* cruel. So you think it is me?"

For a long moment, Wild Boy looked at him. Then he turned away. "No," he said. "You ain't the killer."

"Then who is, Wild Boy? Time is running out for Miss Everett."

Wild Boy breathed in deeply, trying to calm himself. He wished he'd got this wrong, wished there was another solution. But he was certain that he was right.

"I almost didn't work it out," he said. "There was

one clue that got me – the killer's disappearing act in that alley. But once I solved that, everything else made sense. How the hooded man walked, the marks in the mud, that silver hair… In that alley, Clarissa kept saying the hooded man had vanished. But that ain't possible, and there were no secret doors nor drains neither. The killer *must've* been hiding, but there was nowhere to hide. There was just them rats and them boxes. And no one could've hidden in a box, not unless they was really small. Someone like a boy or a girl…"

Wild Boy's big green eyes were filled with sadness as he turned to face the killer. "Or maybe if they had no legs," he said. "Ain't that right, *Sir Oswald*?"

3 5

Sir Oswald Farley sat on the stumps of his legs, one hand gripping the rope that tethered the big top's chandelier. He didn't look surprised by what Wild Boy had said – that *he* was the hooded man, that *he* was the killer.

This was supposed to be a moment of triumph, but all Wild Boy felt was sadness. He wished that he was wrong. He hated that he was right.

"The answer was right in front of me," he said. "I just couldn't see it, or maybe I didn't want to. You didn't scream when the fire caught your cloak at the Doctor's house. Them marks on the ground – they weren't from a crutch or a cane or hobnail boots. They were from wooden legs. Weren't they, Sir Oswald?"

Around the tent, the Gentlemen turned their pistols from Finch and Mary Everett, and aimed them at Sir Oswald.

A sad smile spread across Sir Oswald's wrinkled cheeks. He turned Finch's knife in his palm. "Master Wild," he said softly. "Look out…"

He whirled with the blade and sliced the rope.

Above the ring, the chandelier plunged down, straight at where Augustus Finch lay on the ground.

"No!" Wild Boy cried.

He grabbed the showman and dragged him to safety just as the chandelier crashed down in an explosion of sparks and sawdust.

The Gentlemen staggered back, coughing and calling out: "He's gone! The killer's gone!"

Now Wild Boy was away too – leaping the wreckage and running out of the back of the big top. This had gone wrong, but he could still save Clarissa. He knew that Sir Oswald had fled to his new machine. That was where he'd find her.

It was eerily quiet behind the circus tent, the clamour of the fairground muffled by the closely parked caravans. The only sound was the rain pounding the ground, and Wild Boy's bare feet splashing in puddles as he ran between the vans. He knew where he'd find Sir Oswald's machine. He should do, he thought, he'd seen it enough times – only back then he'd had no idea what he was really looking at.

He kept running until he reached one of the vans on the far side of the square. Wiping wet hair from his eyes, he looked up at his old home, the freak show. The caravan's sides were still decorated with those garish banners, that beast with glowing eyes and torn clothes. *THE SAVAGE SPECTACLE OF WILD BOY.*

For most of the time that he'd lived here he hadn't regarded himself as anything better than the monster on those banners, a freak only good for being mocked and laughed at by slobs. But he knew now that he was more than that. He had a friend. He had a skill. And he had solved a mystery.

He reached up and tore down a banner.

It was as if he'd opened a treasure chest. The wooden walls were covered with shiny copper and silver tubes, snaking along the sides, over and underneath. Wires connected one tube to another, and were fixed by clips to the axles of the iron wheels. Wild Boy could see now that Sir Oswald's changes to the van weren't for ventilation, or heating either. The whole time he had been building his machine.

"Clarissa?" Wild Boy called.

He swung the van door open, and gasped. Clarissa was inside, tied to the wall by a rope that fed through the wooden slats and with one of the Gentlemen's mechanical crowns fixed by screws to her head. Spiked copper rods jutted from the top of the crown. They were the same rods that had been driven into the tiger's head, and transferred the animal's mind into Doctor Griffin's body. A tangle of wires connected the device to the tubes that crawled over the top of the caravan.

Clarissa yelled into her gag. Her eyes flashed Wild Boy warnings that someone was approaching from behind. But he already knew who was there. He just didn't want it to be true.

Something landed in a puddle by his feet. It was the hooded man's mask. Its porcelain beak curled up into the rain.

"Congratulations," the killer said.

The hooded man stepped from between the caravans. Rain streamed over his sagging hood. "I knew you would solve the mystery," he said. "Master Wild."

Wild Boy turned to face him. He wasn't scared any more. He just felt heavy with sadness. "You don't need to hide no more," he said.

The hooded man slid back the shroud – revealing salt-and-pepper hair, and the wrinkled face of Sir Oswald Farley. "You were wrong about one thing though," Sir Oswald said. "They are not *wooden* legs."

The rest of the cloak fell away. Even though Wild Boy knew what he would see, it still made him step back in shock. Sir Oswald balanced on two iron legs – stilts with narrow metal points, springs for suspension, hinges in place of knees and straps fixing them to the stumps of his thighs.

He smiled at Wild Boy sadly. "Professor Wollstonecraft made them for me."

"You and him were friends," Wild Boy said.

"We drank together some nights," Sir Oswald replied. "He drank too much, and spoke too much.

That was how I learned of the Gentlemen, and his idea of building a new machine. But the Professor refused to build it, refused even to tell me where he hid the plans."

"So you killed him."

"No! Master Wild—"

"Don't call me that!" A wave of anger surged through Wild Boy, washing away his sadness. "My friend called me Master Wild," he seethed. "You ain't that person no more. You're a cold-blooded killer."

Sir Oswald's metal legs clacked against the ground as he came closer. Flecks of spit gathered in the corner of his mouth. "I did not mean to kill anyone," he insisted. "That mask, this cloak... I thought I could scare the Professor into giving me his plans. But you saw; he used his knife against me. It was the same with Doctor Griffin."

Wild Boy edged back, confused. Maybe Sir Oswald was telling the truth, but it didn't matter. "You still set me up," he said.

"I *had* to. I couldn't find the Doctor's secret chamber on my own, or the Gentlemen and their machine. But I knew that you could."

His head sank, and grey hair fell around his face. He looked tired and sad. "I was... I was trying to help you," he said quietly.

"*Help* me?"

"I told you that things could get better, remember? That is why I built this machine. For *us*. We could be normal, Master Wild, like everyone else. And not only you and me, but all the performers in these degrading freak shows. Everyone who knows how it feels to be mocked. To be *reviled*. Twenty-six years ago I lost my legs to a cannon blast at Waterloo. It has been been twenty-six years since I last felt like a human being. I lost my legs for my country, and ever since I have been called a freak."

As he spoke, Sir Oswald crouched and unclipped the metal stilts from the tops of his legs. He laid them on the ground, and sat again on the stumps of his thighs.

His voice cracked with emotion. "And what about you, Master Wild? Just because you happen to look different to other people, that will define your whole life. You will never be anything other than a freak. That was why I built the machine. For *us*, Master Wild. I built it for *us*."

Wild Boy tried not to listen. He glimpsed Clarissa again through the half-open caravan door. He had to do *something*.

"Did you not dream of it?" Sir Oswald said. "When you watched people around the fairground, did you not imagine living their lives? And when you saw the Gentlemen's machine, when you knew that it was real... Did you not want it for yourself?"

Wild Boy shook his head. He had wanted to use the machine, but not any more. "You're wrong," he said. "I ain't just a freak and neither were you. You were my friend."

"I still am, Master Wild."

"Then let her go."

Sir Oswald gave another sad smile. "No, I cannot. I have come too far now. The machine works, and I will hang if I do not use it. And for that, I am afraid I require Miss Everett. You see, I have made some more improvements to our old home…"

He reached up and pulled away another of the banners, and then another, exposing the van's extraordinary skeleton of machinery – a mesh of copper wires and twisting pipes that looked like the heart of the Gentlemen's machine in the Tower.

"This device operates in the same way as their machine," Sir Oswald said. "The wheels generate the electricity, which is channelled into the crowns. I shall wear one crown, Miss Everett the other. Once we travel fast enough, this machine will come to life. My mind will be transferred into her body, and hers into mine."

For the first time, Wild Boy realized that the van's horses were harnessed and ready to ride. He had to get Clarissa out of there *now*.

He burst for the door, but something hard crashed against the back of his skull and he collapsed to the ground. He tried to get up, but his head whirled and he slumped back. Through the rain and dizziness, he saw that he'd been struck by one of Sir Oswald's metal legs.

Sir Oswald came closer, walking on his hands. Carefully, kindly, he raised Wild Boy's head and slid his cloak beneath. "I am truly sorry, Master Wild," he said. "I never wished to hurt you."

He climbed up into the driver's perch and fastened the other mechanical crown to his head. Wires trailed from the device into the caravan behind him – into his machine. "I hope we will meet again, old friend. And when we do, I will look very different."

Sir Oswald lashed the horses, and the machine began to move.

"No…" Wild Boy groaned. "Please…"

He struggled up and staggered after them, but he was too slow. As the machine rumbled onto the street, it gathered pace. Its pipes and wires began to crackle and glow, turning white with heat and then blue with electrical fire.

"Clarissa!" Wild Boy yelled.

"Ya! Ya!" cried a voice.

Wild Boy dived aside as another carriage burst into the street. He was stunned to see that it was the Lord Mayor's golden coach, and Marcus was driving it. The Gentleman slowed the carriage down as he waited for him to catch up. "Hurry!"

As soon as Wild Boy was inside, Marcus lashed the reins and they were away again, racing through the rain – after Sir Oswald, after Clarissa, after the machine.

36

"That's him! Go faster!"

Wild Boy tumbled back onto the seat as the Lord Mayor's coach jolted over cracks in the road. Two wheels came off the ground and the carriage almost tipped over before slamming back to the broken surface.

Drunken crowds ran screaming from the street. A chestnut seller dived out of the way, only to see his tin stove crushed like paper beneath the coach's wheels. Sparks flew, but Marcus wasn't slowing down. The coach tore through a washing line, smashed down a shop sign, ripped through a pile of newspapers. Front pages flapped up into the rain, screaming *WILD BOY AND CLARISSA STILL AT LARGE!*

"Ya! Ya!"

Rain whipped Wild Boy's face as he leaned from the window. He could just see his old caravan, a hundred yards ahead. No, not a caravan – it was a machine on wheels. Electricity crackled along the pipes and wires that criss-crossed its wooden walls. The iron wheels scattered sparks in their path. Sir Oswald sat in the driver's perch, connected to the machine by one of the mechanical crowns.

"The machine," Marcus said. "It's starting to work."

Wild Boy felt useless, helpless. All he could do was watch as the machine grew even brighter, streaking blue light in its wake. What was happening to Clarissa in there?

"The bridge!" he cried. "He's heading for the bridge!"

The narrow street widened into the broad thoroughfare of London Bridge. Workers downed tools and fled as the two vehicles clattered towards them. Sir Oswald's machine hit a pickaxe, slowing it down for vital moments. Seizing his chance, Marcus urged his horses on until the carriages were racing side by side, separated by a line of builder's blocks that ran along the middle of the bridge.

Wild Boy *had* to stop that van. And he could think of only one way.

He slid across the coach and pushed open the window. Orange blurs of gaslight streaked past as the carriage sped along the bridge. He didn't let himself stop and think about what he was doing. In one quick move he pulled himself out through the window.

Wind and driving rain threatened to tear him off the side of the coach. But he clung tight to the golden frame and climbed up onto the roof.

"Marcus!" he shouted. "Get closer to the machine!"

Marcus pulled the reins, steering the Mayor's coach even closer to the centre of the bridge. Two wheels scraped the stone divide, spraying sparks. This was as near as they could get but they were still yards away.

Wild Boy glimpsed himself in the reflection of the machine's pipes. He looked every bit as terrified as he felt. But he remembered the look in Clarissa's eyes when he'd struck her in the Tower, and the promise he'd made to save her.

He jumped.

"AAAAGH!"

He landed hard on top of the machine. He tried to grasp one of the pipes, but the speed flipped him sideways. His head hit wood as he fell over the side. Only his foot, caught between the pipes as he fell, saved him from tumbling to the street. He swung across the side of the machine, so close to the grinding wheel that it shaved the hair on his cheek.

The machine glowed brighter. The pipes throbbed. The wires fizzed.

Wild Boy felt the heat burn his coat and scorch the hair on his back. The van door swung open and he saw Clarissa inside, her pale face shining blue in the machine's electrical storm. She'd managed to shake off her gag but she remained tied to the wall, with the crown screwed to her head. She stopped struggling, surprised to see Wild Boy hanging upside down outside the door.

"Help me then!" she screamed.

"I'm trying!" Wild Boy replied.

Struggling against the wind, he reached up and gripped one of the van's wooden slats. His hand brushed a pipe, and a shock of electricity shot down his arm. But he fought away the pain and pulled himself back onto the roof.

Now that he was close to Sir Oswald, Wild Boy didn't know what to do. Just a few days ago, this man had been his friend. Was it true what he'd said – that he had not meant to kill the Professor or Doctor Griffin?

It didn't matter. He just had to stop this machine.

He leaned forward and took hold of the wires that trailed from Sir Oswald's crown. And then he yanked. He hoped to tear them from the device, severing its connection to Clarissa. But Sir Oswald's head swung back and caught the edge of the van roof, knocking him out cold. His hands slipped from the reins and he slumped forward.

"Get up!" Wild Boy yelled at him.

He reached past him and grabbed one of the reins. But the horses were too scared to slow down. They ran even faster, out of control.

Marcus tried to steer the Mayor's coach closer but

couldn't pass the stone barrier. "Get Miss Everett out of there!" he shouted.

Edging back, Wild Boy pulled open the hatch in the roof and slid through. He dropped straight down and landed inside the van.

"What are you doing?" Clarissa cried.

"It's a rescue…"

"*Rescue?* We're going to crash! Why did you take so long?"

Wild Boy grunted – there was no pleasing some people. Dragging himself up, he began to unscrew the crown from around Clarrisa's head. He lifted it away and untied the ropes that bound her to the wall. The van shook as its wheels crashed against the blocks in the road.

"Hurry!" Clarissa said.

"I *am* hurrying!"

"Hurry faster!"

The van jolted again, harder. "What was that?" Clarissa said, as she pulled free of the ropes.

Wild Boy pushed the van door open and looked outside. "The horses! They've broken free!"

The animals had jumped the stone barrier that divided the bridge, but the machine hadn't followed. Its wheels crashed against the blocks, and now it was on its own, trailing sparks through the rain. At any moment it could plunge from the bridge.

"We have to jump," Clarissa said.

Marcus drove his coach as close as possible to the

runaway machine. If Wild Boy and Clarissa were lucky, they could leap and cling on to its railings.

"Go!" Wild Boy yelled.

Clarissa jumped. Instinct guided her hands – she caught the golden frame of the Mayor's coach, flung the door open and swung inside. "Come on!" she called.

Wild Boy was about to follow, but he glanced back. The hatch to the driver's perch was open, and he saw Sir Oswald unconscious in his seat. He couldn't just leave him.

"No," Clarissa said. "Wild Boy, don't!"

But he was already back inside the van, reaching through the hatch for his old friend. "Sir Oswald!" he shouted. "Wake up!"

Too late. The van's wheels hit the rubble where workers had been repairing the edge of the bridge. Wild Boy tumbled back as the machine flipped over and crashed onto its side in a burst of sparks. It skidded across the surface … and came to a shuddering halt half-on and half-off the bridge.

The pipes groaned, glowing paler as the electricity in the machine died out.

The van creaked, wobbled. Inside, Wild Boy lay at the wrong end of the see-saw, staring up at the open caravan door. Rain poured through, hissing against hot metal. He didn't dare move, terrified that whatever he did would send the van over the edge.

"Master Wild…"

The driver's hatch hung open. Sir Oswald sat in his perch, held in by a strap over the stumps of his thighs. The machine's crown had slipped on his head. He looked like a sad, broken king on his throne.

He stared down at the dark river. He knew that it was his weight that was tipping the van over the edge. His hands shook as he reached to unfasten the strap.

"I am sorry, Master Wild," he said. "I am sorry for everything."

"No, Sir Oswald. Don't…"

"All I wanted was to help you. Just tell me you believe that."

Wild Boy did, and he said so. Despite everything his friend had done, he didn't want him to die. "Please, Sir Oswald. You don't have to do this."

Sir Oswald looked back through the hatch. Tears glistened in his eyes, but he managed one last smile for his old friend. "Poppycock," he said.

He unfastened the strap, and fell.

Sir Oswald didn't scream, didn't make a sound other than the splash from hitting the water. The scream came from Wild Boy – a desperate, heart-broken cry that filled the van and shook its walls as he watched the river swallow his friend. But, at the same time, he'd never felt so strong. Sir Oswald had done that for him – so now, more than ever, he was determined to survive.

The caravan tipped back towards the bridge but still threatened to slide over the edge. The open door was right above him. He had to get through and leap to safety.

Now, he urged himself. *Now!*

He sprang up and reached for the door. He managed to grasp the edge, but the caravan swung from the bridge. It slid over the side and plummeted down...

Wild Boy cried out, but he didn't fall with the van. Instead he remained hanging in the air. At first he didn't understand what had happened. Then he looked up and yelled in delight.

A pale face smiled down at him, dotted with bright freckles. Clarissa dangled upside down from a rope, its other end held by Marcus on the bridge above. She'd jumped from the bridge, catching Wild Boy's hand as the van fell.

Her grin spread wider. "*This* is a rescue," she said.

Slowly Marcus hauled them up, until they both stood safely on the bridge. Wild Boy shook all over from his brush with death, the pain in his shoulder, and his grief that Sir Oswald was gone.

But he had kept his promise. Exhausted, he leaned against Clarissa, each propping the other up. Fiery red hair tumbled over burnt brown ones.

They heard whistles and shouts as police officers charged along the bridge. But they were too tired to run. Besides, Wild Boy had had enough of running.

Over Clarissa's shoulder he looked at Marcus. The golden-eyed man slicked back his silver hair and replied with the slightest of smiles. And Wild Boy knew that everything would be all right.

He leaned into Clarissa and closed his eyes.

37

Wild Boy opened his eyes.

He was lying in a bed – a proper soft bed with clean linen and a plump feather pillow that smelled of lavender. His chest ached as he shifted up against the headboard. A bandage was wrapped around his side, and his arm hung in a tight sling. Sunlight streamed through a window, dazzling his eyes.

Marcus Bishop stood over him, leaning on his cane even more heavily than before. In his other hand was a thick sheaf of papers.

"So," he said, "did you have fun at the fair?"

Wild Boy grimaced. He was in no mood for jokes. He looked around the room, trying to make sense of his surroundings. It was bright, breezy and spotlessly clean, unlike any room he'd been in before. There was a cupboard that was gilded with gold, a chest that looked like solid silver. Through the door, he glimpsed oil paintings on the walls. He heard the clip-clop of horses and the clatter of carriages on a street some way away.

"Am I in a *palace*?" he asked.

Marcus poured him a glass of water from a jug. "You have been asleep for twenty-four hours," he said. "Drink."

The glass trembled in Wild Boy's hand as he took several small sips. He was surprised to see that his fingernails had been scrubbed clean. Someone had taken great care in washing him, but he could still smell sewage…

"Sir Oswald?" he asked. "Did he die?"

Marcus's jaw tightened. "Almost certainly."

"And his machine?"

"It joined the killer on the riverbed."

Killer. It seemed strange to call Sir Oswald that. Wild Boy knew that, in the end, his old friend had saved his life. He didn't feel angry at him – he felt sad that he was gone. Without him the world felt emptier.

"What about me?" he asked. "Them blasted coppers still after me?"

"That has been taken care of. In fact, them blasted coppers would rather appreciate your assistance."

Marcus flicked through a few of his papers. "An interesting new case. Four murders, all Members of Parliament, killed in their homes. The killer sends notes to the police, informing them of the exact date and time that the next crime will occur. He is always correct, to the second. His next target is the Prime Minister, and the police are at a loss. And when the police are at a loss, they come to us."

Wild Boy took another sip of water. His neck ached but he felt surprisingly awake.

"Arrest the clock-maker," he said.

Marcus looked at him for a long moment, and a smile broke across his face. He tucked the papers under his arm. "Care to come along?"

"I ain't one of you, you know? I ain't no bloomin' Gentleman."

"But you will come anyway." Marcus limped from the room, holding up the papers. "There are puzzles to be solved."

Wild Boy slumped back in the bed. He hated how that man always knew what he was thinking. He hated too that he was always right. He *would* go with him. Not because he had nowhere else to go, but because he wanted to. People to spy on, puzzles to solve, new places to snoop around...

He felt it in the hairs all over his body – *excitement*.

He lay back, enjoying the warm sun and the cool breeze on his face. "I know you're there," he said. "In the cupboard."

The cupboard door creaked open. An angry eye glared from the dark.

"How *could* you know?" Clarissa said from inside.

He'd known she was there from the moment he

had woken. But he also knew that it would annoy her if he didn't say how, so he just shrugged.

Clarissa stepped gingerly from the cupboard, still aching from their adventure. She had got rid of her circus costume and was dressed entirely in black – black hood, black trousers, long black coat. But her hair blazed like fire in the sunlight, and her freckles looked like they'd been painted onto her face with strawberry juice.

She came up to the bed and they looked at each other for a long moment. They were both struggling not to smile, still trying to look tough.

"I ain't not forgiven you, you know?" Clarissa said.

"Don't care anyhow," Wild Boy replied.

Clarissa peered out of the door, making sure they were alone. A mischievous smile creased across her cheeks. "Look at this."

She dug in her pocket and brought out a golden necklace studded with emeralds and rubies. The gleaming jewels dazzled Wild Boy's eyes.

"Where did you get that?" he asked.

"I stole it. Don't you know where we *are*?" She stuffed the necklace back in her coat. "They want us to work for them, you know. The Gentlemen. They need us cos they're too stupid to solve their own mysteries. I told Marcus we would. We will, won't we?"

"Yeah… Maybe."

Really Wild Boy was bursting to get involved. It wasn't just Marcus's cases that intrigued him, but the Gentlemen too. He wanted to find out more about them, to uncover their secrets.

"Marcus pretends to be mean," Clarissa said, "but I think he's all right. Remember I said that you can't pick a Smithson lock with a nail? Well, he can! Said he'd teach me."

She turned and gazed out of the window. "At the fair," she said quietly. "Did you see my mother?"

"Yes, I did."

"Did she… Did she speak about me?"

Wild Boy remembered her mother's cruel words in the circus tent, but decided not to tell Clarissa. Mary Everett had already hurt his friend enough. He wouldn't let her do so any more. "I'm sorry," he said. "She didn't say anything."

Clarissa was silent for a moment, a slender silhouette against the window. "I'm sorry I called you a freak," she said.

Wild Boy couldn't fight his smile any longer. "I'm sorry I called you normal," he replied.

Now she grinned too. She punched him on the arm. "Hurry up," she said. "Marcus says we're going to catch another killer!" Then she rushed from the room.

Wild Boy knew he needed to rest for longer, but he didn't want to miss out on the fun. He slid from the bed and began putting on the clothes that hung for him in the cupboard – a new pair of breeches, a crisp white shirt and a red military coat with gold tasselled buttons – swearing loudly each time he discovered a new pain in his bruised limbs.

Fully dressed, he considered his reflection in the window. The coat was just like his old one except that it was brand new, tailor-made just for him. It felt like an old friend.

It was a perfect fit.

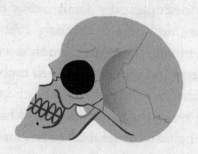

ABOUT THE AUTHOR

Rob Lloyd Jones never wanted to be a writer when he grew up – he wanted to be Indiana Jones. So he studied Egyptology and archaeology and went on trips to faraway places. But all he found were interesting stories so he decided to write them down. *Wild Boy* is Rob's first novel, although he has written more than thirty other books for children, including non-fiction and adaptations of such classics as *Jekyll and Hyde*.

About writing *Wild Boy*, he says, "I won't lie – *Wild Boy* began with Sherlock Holmes. I adore detective stories, and always wanted to write one. But I'd never found a reason for my hero to be a detective, other than just because. Then I read the wonderful *Seventy Years a Showman*, by legendary Victorian circus owner Lord George Sanger. (He wasn't really a lord; he gave himself that title.) Sanger recalled

LOOK OUT FOR **BOOK 2**

WILD BOY
★ & THE ★
BLACK
TERROR

A POISONER WHO STRIKES WITHOUT TRACE, LEAVING VICTIMS MAD WITH *terror*... AND THEN DEAD.

IS THERE A CURE FOR THE BLACK TERROR?

To find out, Wild Boy and Clarissa must catch the killer. Their hunt will lead them from the city's vilest slums to its grandest palaces, and to a darkness at the heart of its very highest society.

WILD BOY AND THE BLACK TERROR   ·   ISBN: 978 1 4063 4140 9 the gritty, sometimes gory details of life in travelling freak shows, and I got to thinking. What if one of those performers spent their days locked up, spying on the fairground though cracks in caravan walls? What if that person learned to tell people's tales just through tiny details he spotted? What if he had this amazing skill but he didn't even know it? And I knew I had to write his story. But, also, this book is a love song to London, my home. Most of its events take place along the route of my walk into work, where they happened around me in fun and frightening daydreams."

Rob lives in London with his wife and young son, who has big eyes like Wild Boy but is not as hairy.

VISIT ROB AT

WWW·ROBLLOYDJONES·COM/WILDBOY